Billy & Buddy

Roba

FRiENDS FiRST

Original title: Boule & Bill 3 – Les copains d'abord

Original edition: © Studio Boule & Bill, 2008
by Roba

English translation: © 2012 Cinebook Ltd

Translator: Erica Jeffrey
Lettering and text layout: Imadjinn
Printed in Spain by Just Colour Graphic

This edition first published in Great Britain in 2012 by
Cinebook Ltd
56 Beech Avenue
Canterbury, Kent
CT4 7TA
www.cinebook.com

A CIP catalogue record for this book
is available from the British Library

ISBN 978-1-84918-124-2

9th CINEBOOK
The 9th Art Publisher

Return to Sender

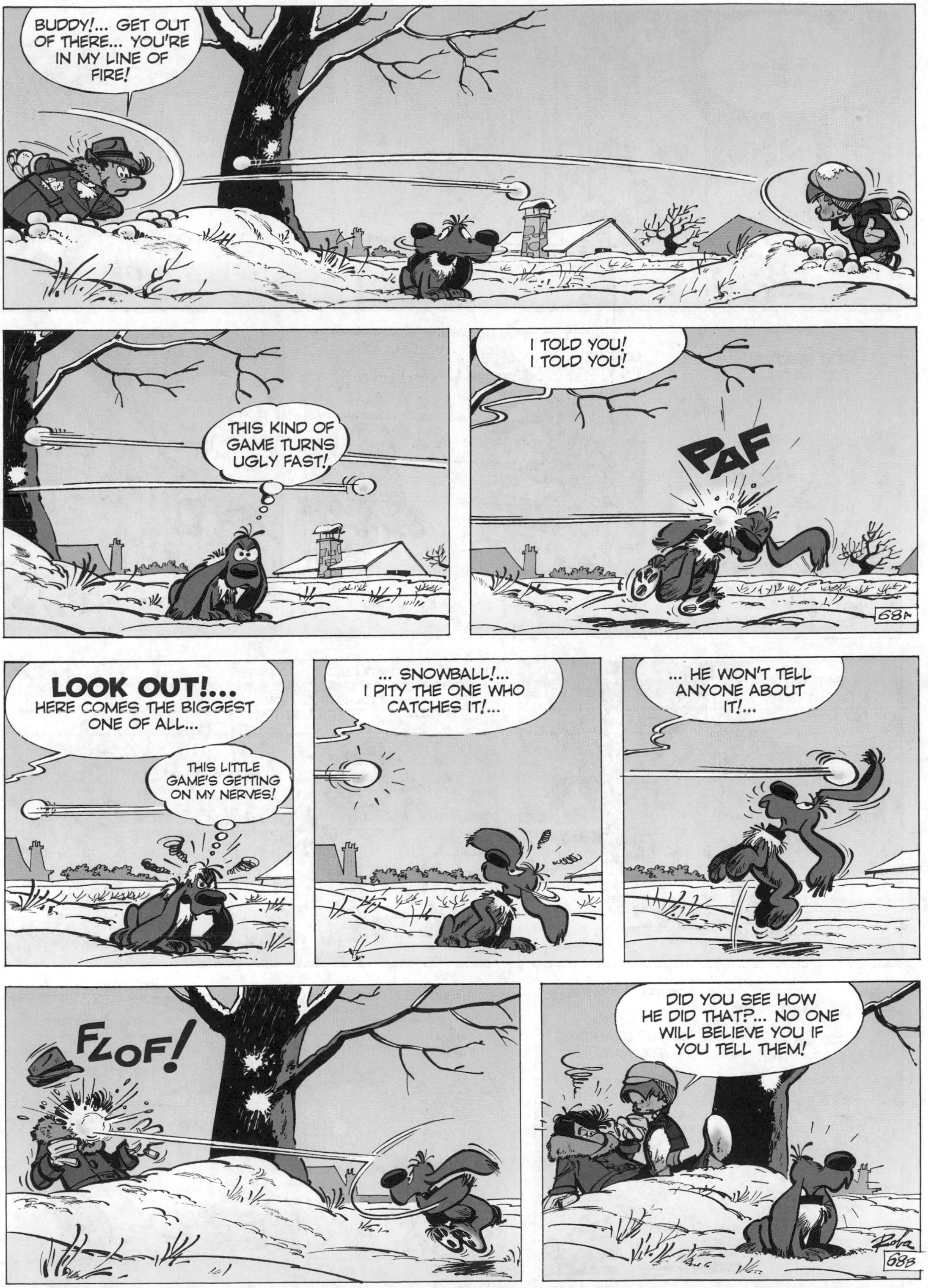

BUDDY!... GET OUT OF THERE... YOU'RE IN MY LINE OF FIRE!
THIS KIND OF GAME TURNS UGLY FAST!
I TOLD YOU! I TOLD YOU!
PAF
68A
LOOK OUT!... HERE COMES THE BIGGEST ONE OF ALL...
THIS LITTLE GAME'S GETTING ON MY NERVES!
... SNOWBALL!... I PITY THE ONE WHO CATCHES IT!...
... HE WON'T TELL ANYONE ABOUT IT!...
FLOF!
DID YOU SEE HOW HE DID THAT?... NO ONE WILL BELIEVE YOU IF YOU TELL THEM!
Roba
68B

Some Christmas this is!

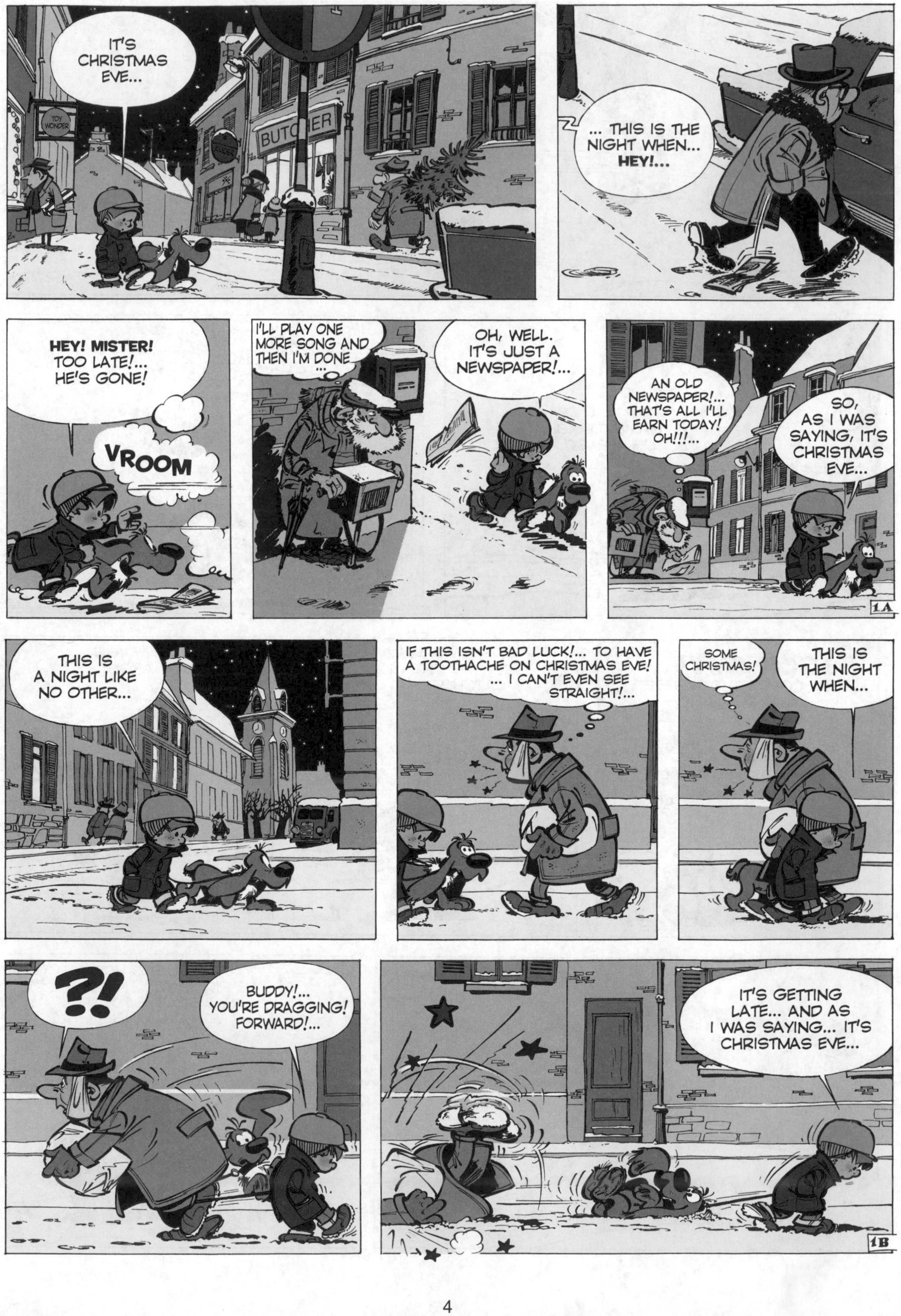
IT'S CHRISTMAS EVE...
TOY WONDER
BUTCHER
... THIS IS THE NIGHT WHEN... HEY!...
HEY! MISTER! TOO LATE!... HE'S GONE!
VROOM
I'LL PLAY ONE MORE SONG AND THEN I'M DONE ...
OH, WELL. IT'S JUST A NEWSPAPER!...
AN OLD NEWSPAPER!... THAT'S ALL I'LL EARN TODAY! OH!!!...
SO, AS I WAS SAYING, IT'S CHRISTMAS EVE...
1A
THIS IS A NIGHT LIKE NO OTHER...
IF THIS ISN'T BAD LUCK!... TO HAVE A TOOTHACHE ON CHRISTMAS EVE! ... I CAN'T EVEN SEE STRAIGHT!...
SOME CHRISTMAS!
THIS IS THE NIGHT WHEN...
?!
BUDDY!... YOU'RE DRAGGING! FORWARD!...
IT'S GETTING LATE... AND AS I WAS SAYING... IT'S CHRISTMAS EVE...
1B

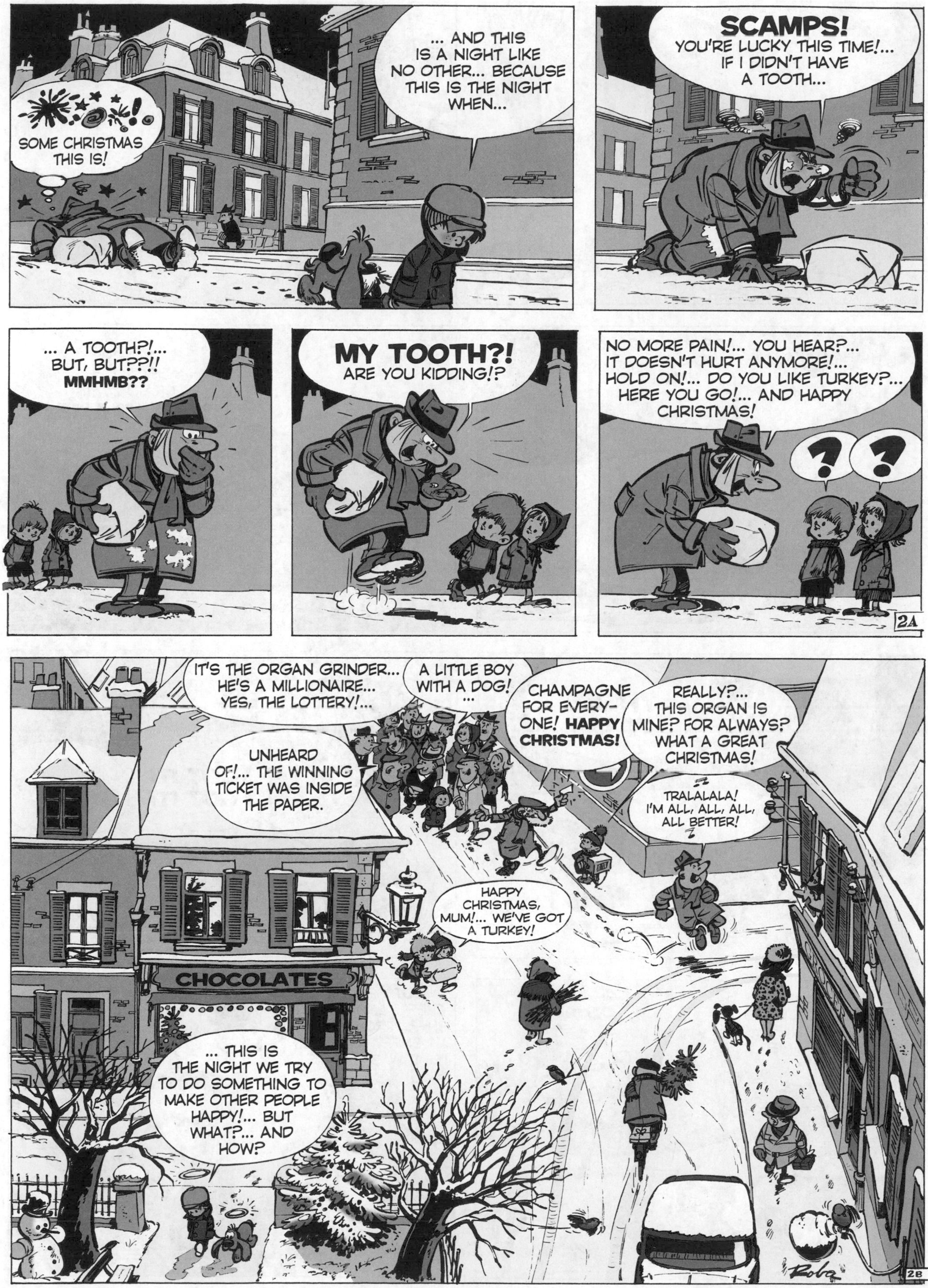
SOME CHRISTMAS THIS IS!
... AND THIS IS A NIGHT LIKE NO OTHER... BECAUSE THIS IS THE NIGHT WHEN...
SCAMPS! YOU'RE LUCKY THIS TIME!... IF I DIDN'T HAVE A TOOTH...
... A TOOTH?!... BUT, BUT??!! MMHMB??
MY TOOTH?! ARE YOU KIDDING!?
NO MORE PAIN!... YOU HEAR?... IT DOESN'T HURT ANYMORE!... HOLD ON!... DO YOU LIKE TURKEY?... HERE YOU GO!... AND HAPPY CHRISTMAS!
??
2A
IT'S THE ORGAN GRINDER... HE'S A MILLIONAIRE... YES, THE LOTTERY!...
A LITTLE BOY WITH A DOG! ...
CHAMPAGNE FOR EVERY-ONE! HAPPY CHRISTMAS!
REALLY?... THIS ORGAN IS MINE? FOR ALWAYS? WHAT A GREAT CHRISTMAS!
UNHEARD OF!... THE WINNING TICKET WAS INSIDE THE PAPER.
TRALALALA! I'M ALL, ALL, ALL, ALL BETTER!
HAPPY CHRISTMAS, MUM!... WE'VE GOT A TURKEY!
CHOCOLATES
... THIS IS THE NIGHT WE TRY TO DO SOMETHING TO MAKE OTHER PEOPLE HAPPY!... BUT WHAT?... AND HOW?

Sealing the Deal

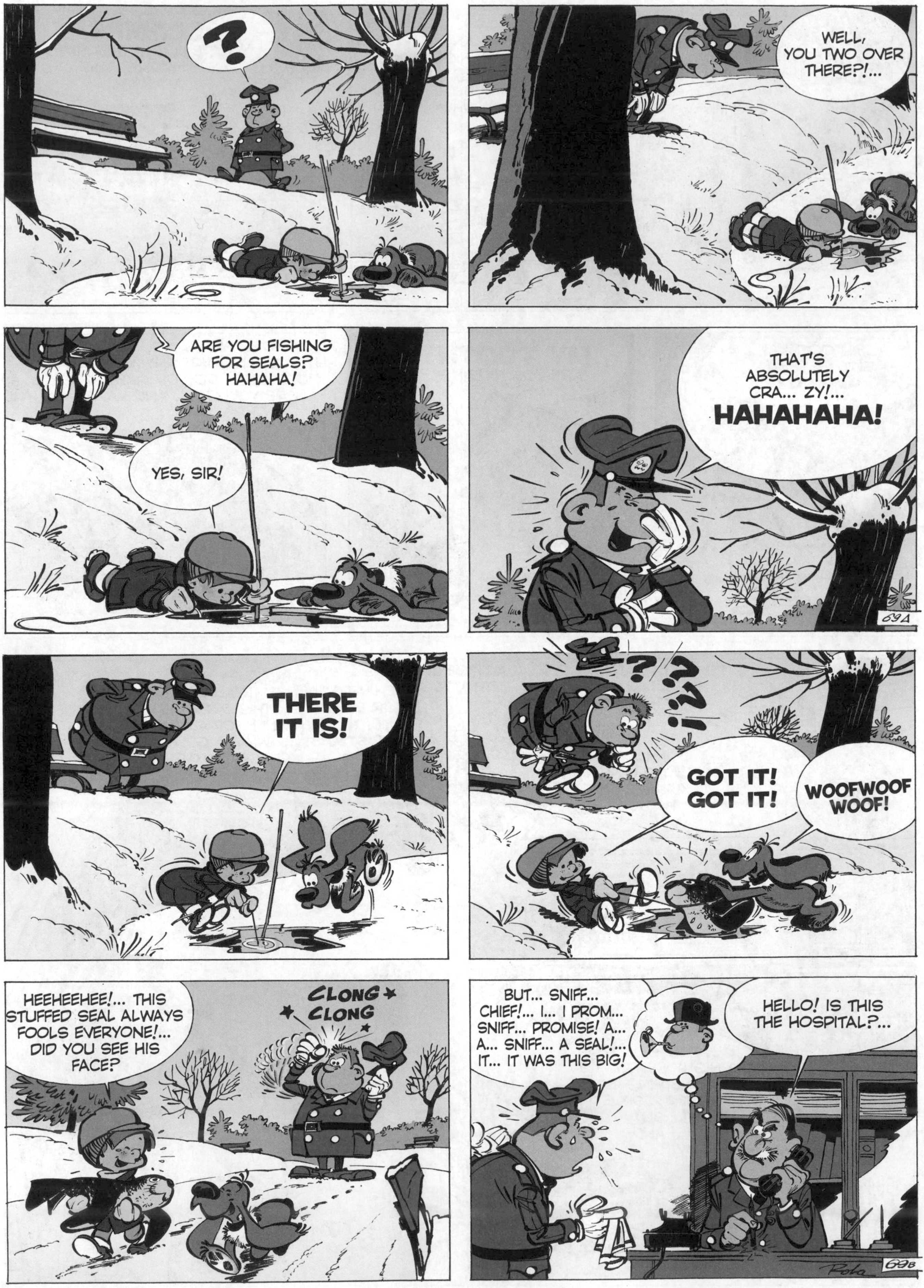
?
WELL, YOU TWO OVER THERE?!...
ARE YOU FISHING FOR SEALS? HAHAHA!
YES, SIR!
THAT'S ABSOLUTELY CRA... ZY!... HAHAHAHA!
69A
THERE IT IS!
? ?!?!
GOT IT! GOT IT!
WOOFWOOF WOOF!
HEEHEEHEE!... THIS STUFFED SEAL ALWAYS FOOLS EVERYONE!... DID YOU SEE HIS FACE?
CLONG CLONG
BUT... SNIFF... CHIEF!... I... I PROM... SNIFF... PROMISE! A... A... SNIFF... A SEAL!... IT... IT WAS THIS BIG!
HELLO! IS THIS THE HOSPITAL?...
Roba
69B

A Good Save

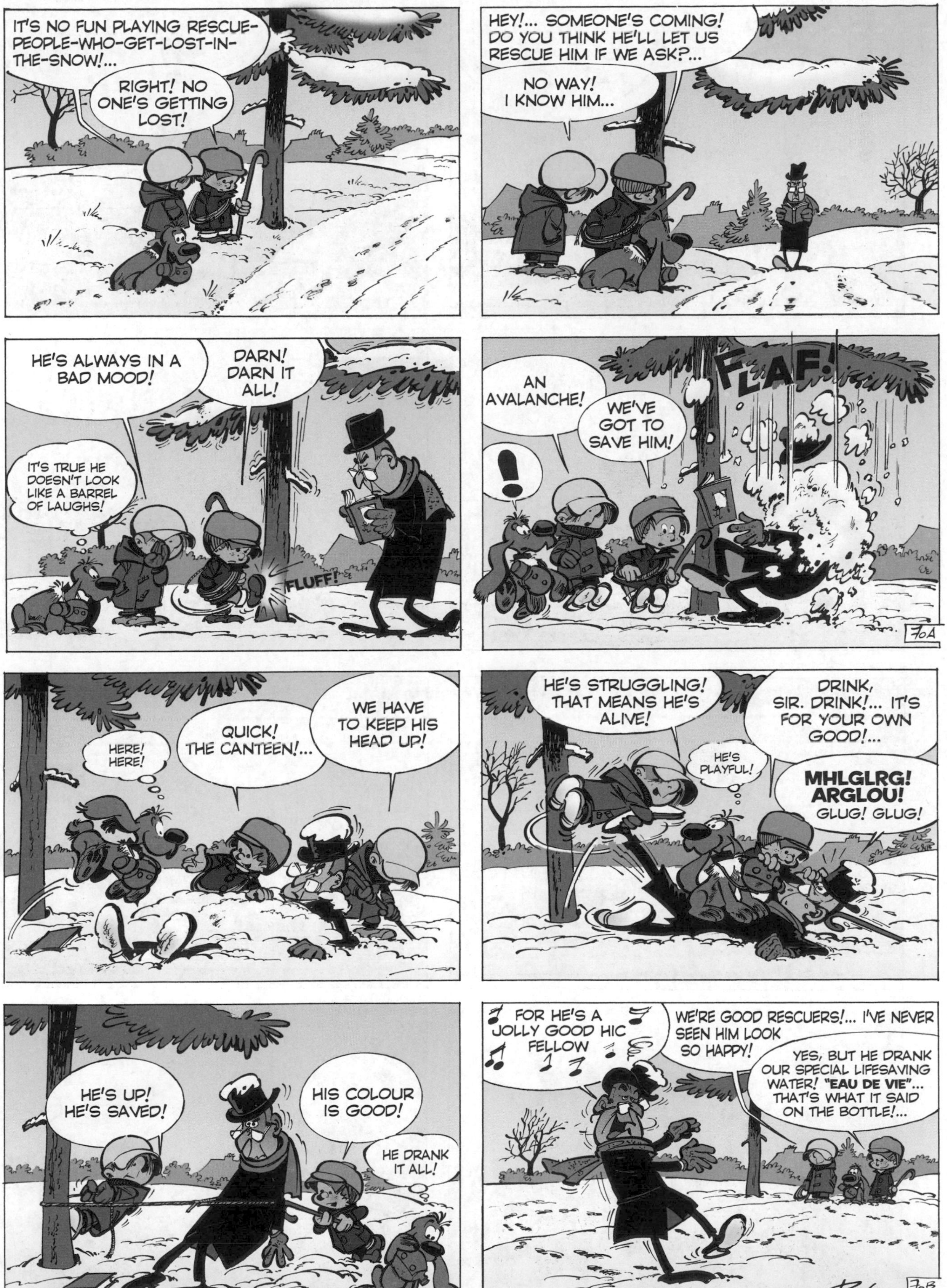

IT'S NO FUN PLAYING RESCUE-PEOPLE-WHO-GET-LOST-IN-THE-SNOW!...
RIGHT! NO ONE'S GETTING LOST!
HEY!... SOMEONE'S COMING! DO YOU THINK HE'LL LET US RESCUE HIM IF WE ASK?...
NO WAY! I KNOW HIM...
HE'S ALWAYS IN A BAD MOOD!
DARN! DARN IT ALL!
IT'S TRUE HE DOESN'T LOOK LIKE A BARREL OF LAUGHS!
FLUFF!
AN AVALANCHE!
WE'VE GOT TO SAVE HIM!
FLAF!
HERE! HERE!
QUICK! THE CANTEEN!...
WE HAVE TO KEEP HIS HEAD UP!
HE'S STRUGGLING! THAT MEANS HE'S ALIVE!
HE'S PLAYFUL!
DRINK, SIR. DRINK!... IT'S FOR YOUR OWN GOOD!...
MHLGLRG! ARGLOU! GLUG! GLUG!
HE'S UP! HE'S SAVED!
HIS COLOUR IS GOOD!
HE DRANK IT ALL!
FOR HE'S A JOLLY GOOD HIC FELLOW
WE'RE GOOD RESCUERS!... I'VE NEVER SEEN HIM LOOK SO HAPPY!
YES, BUT HE DRANK OUR SPECIAL LIFESAVING WATER! "EAU DE VIE"... THAT'S WHAT IT SAID ON THE BOTTLE!...
Roba

The Freeloaders

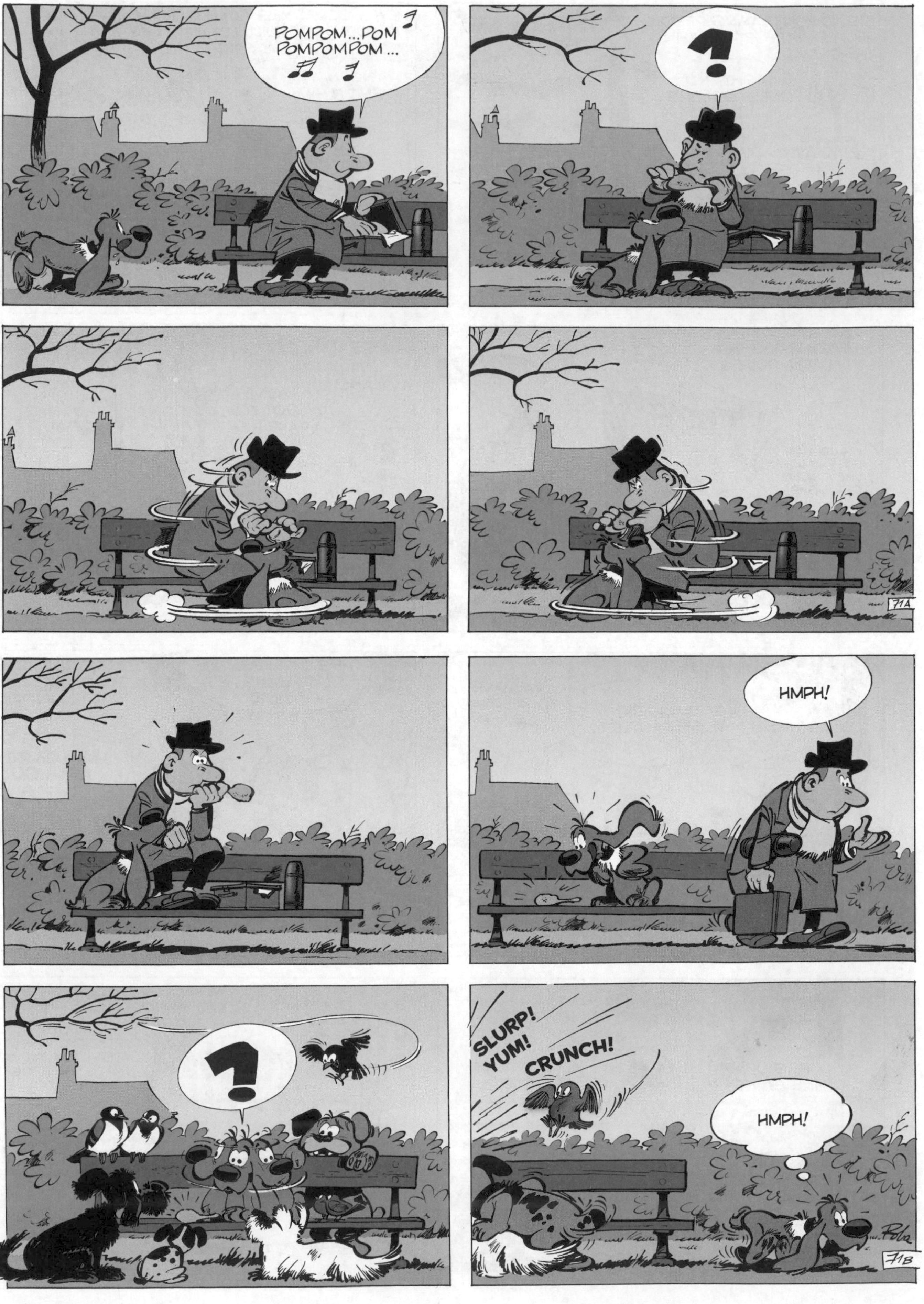
POMPOM...POM POMPOMPOM...
?
HMPH!
?
SLURP!
YUM!
CRUNCH!
HMPH!

Dognapper

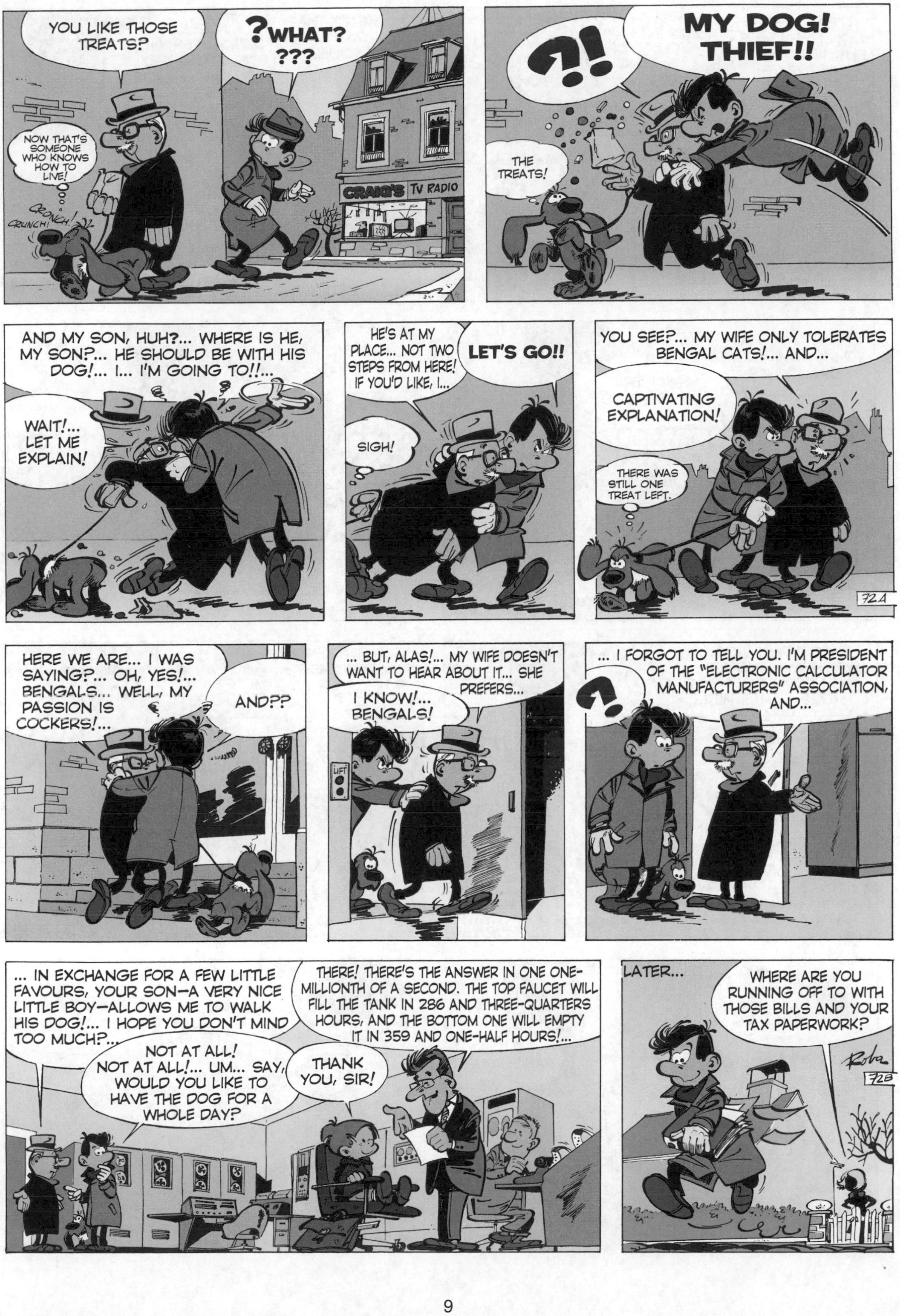

YOU LIKE THOSE TREATS?
NOW THAT'S SOMEONE WHO KNOWS HOW TO LIVE!
CRONCH! CRUNCH!
?WHAT? ???
CRAIG'S TV RADIO
?!
MY DOG! THIEF!!
THE TREATS!
AND MY SON, HUH?... WHERE IS HE, MY SON?... HE SHOULD BE WITH HIS DOG!... I... I'M GOING TO!!...
WAIT!... LET ME EXPLAIN!
HE'S AT MY PLACE... NOT TWO STEPS FROM HERE! IF YOU'D LIKE, I...
LET'S GO!!
SIGH!
YOU SEE?... MY WIFE ONLY TOLERATES BENGAL CATS!... AND...
CAPTIVATING EXPLANATION!
THERE WAS STILL ONE TREAT LEFT.
72A
HERE WE ARE... I WAS SAYING?... OH, YES!... BENGALS... WELL, MY PASSION IS COCKERS!...
AND??
... BUT, ALAS!... MY WIFE DOESN'T WANT TO HEAR ABOUT IT... SHE PREFERS...
I KNOW!... BENGALS!
LIFT
... I FORGOT TO TELL YOU. I'M PRESIDENT OF THE "ELECTRONIC CALCULATOR MANUFACTURERS" ASSOCIATION, AND...
?
... IN EXCHANGE FOR A FEW LITTLE FAVOURS, YOUR SON—A VERY NICE LITTLE BOY—ALLOWS ME TO WALK HIS DOG!... I HOPE YOU DON'T MIND TOO MUCH?...
NOT AT ALL! NOT AT ALL!... UM... SAY, WOULD YOU LIKE TO HAVE THE DOG FOR A WHOLE DAY?
THERE! THERE'S THE ANSWER IN ONE ONE-MILLIONTH OF A SECOND. THE TOP FAUCET WILL FILL THE TANK IN 286 AND THREE-QUARTERS HOURS, AND THE BOTTOM ONE WILL EMPTY IT IN 359 AND ONE-HALF HOURS!...
THANK YOU, SIR!
LATER...
WHERE ARE YOU RUNNING OFF TO WITH THOSE BILLS AND YOUR TAX PAPERWORK?
Roba
72B

The Law of Gravity

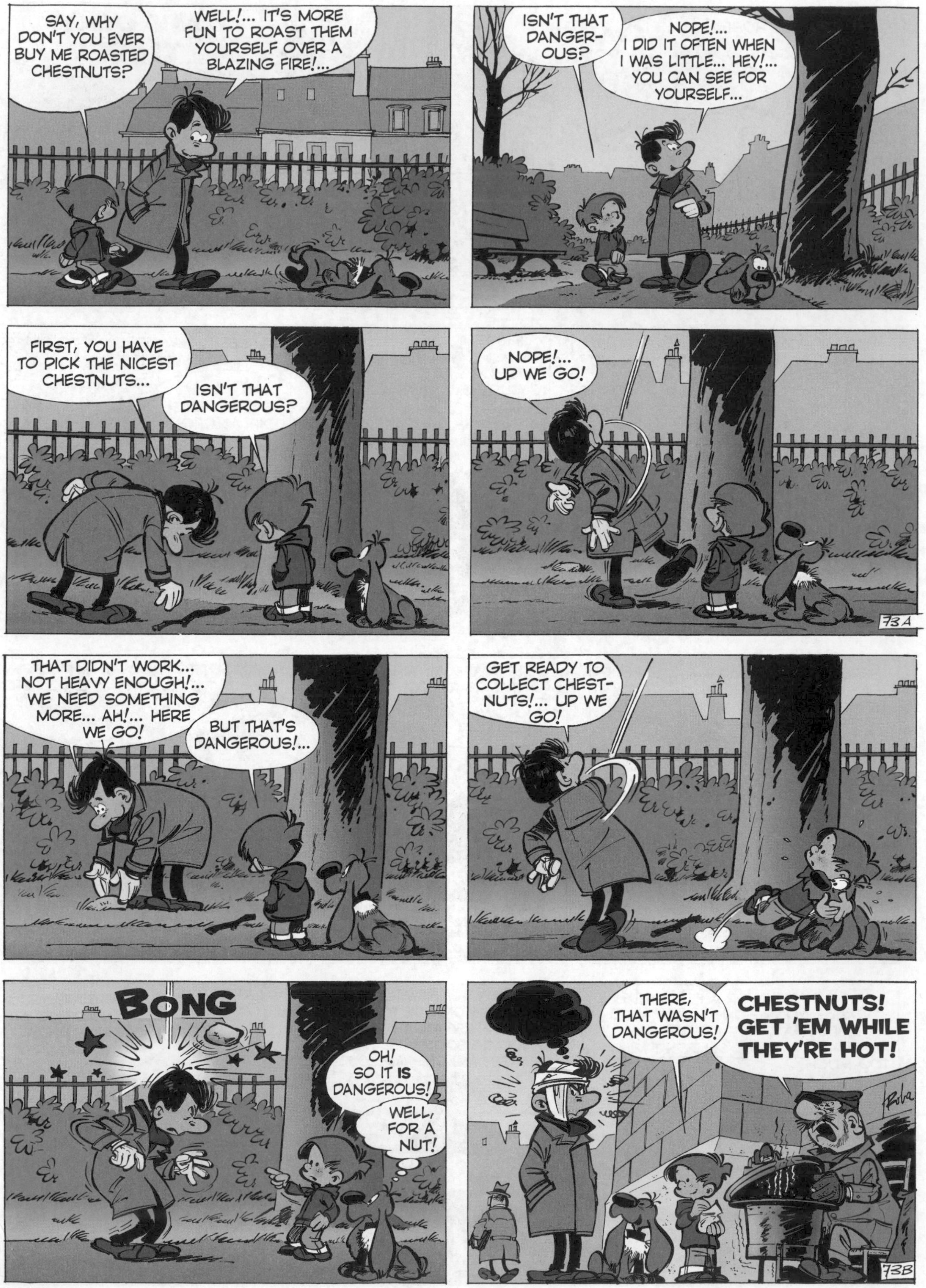

SAY, WHY DON'T YOU EVER BUY ME ROASTED CHESTNUTS?
WELL!... IT'S MORE FUN TO ROAST THEM YOURSELF OVER A BLAZING FIRE!...
ISN'T THAT DANGER-OUS?
NOPE!... I DID IT OFTEN WHEN I WAS LITTLE... HEY!... YOU CAN SEE FOR YOURSELF...
FIRST, YOU HAVE TO PICK THE NICEST CHESTNUTS...
ISN'T THAT DANGEROUS?
NOPE!... UP WE GO!
73A
THAT DIDN'T WORK... NOT HEAVY ENOUGH!... WE NEED SOMETHING MORE... AH!... HERE WE GO!
BUT THAT'S DANGEROUS!...
GET READY TO COLLECT CHEST-NUTS!... UP WE GO!
BONG
OH! SO IT IS DANGEROUS!
WELL, FOR A NUT!
THERE, THAT WASN'T DANGEROUS!
CHESTNUTS! GET 'EM WHILE THEY'RE HOT!
Roba
73B

Punching Bag

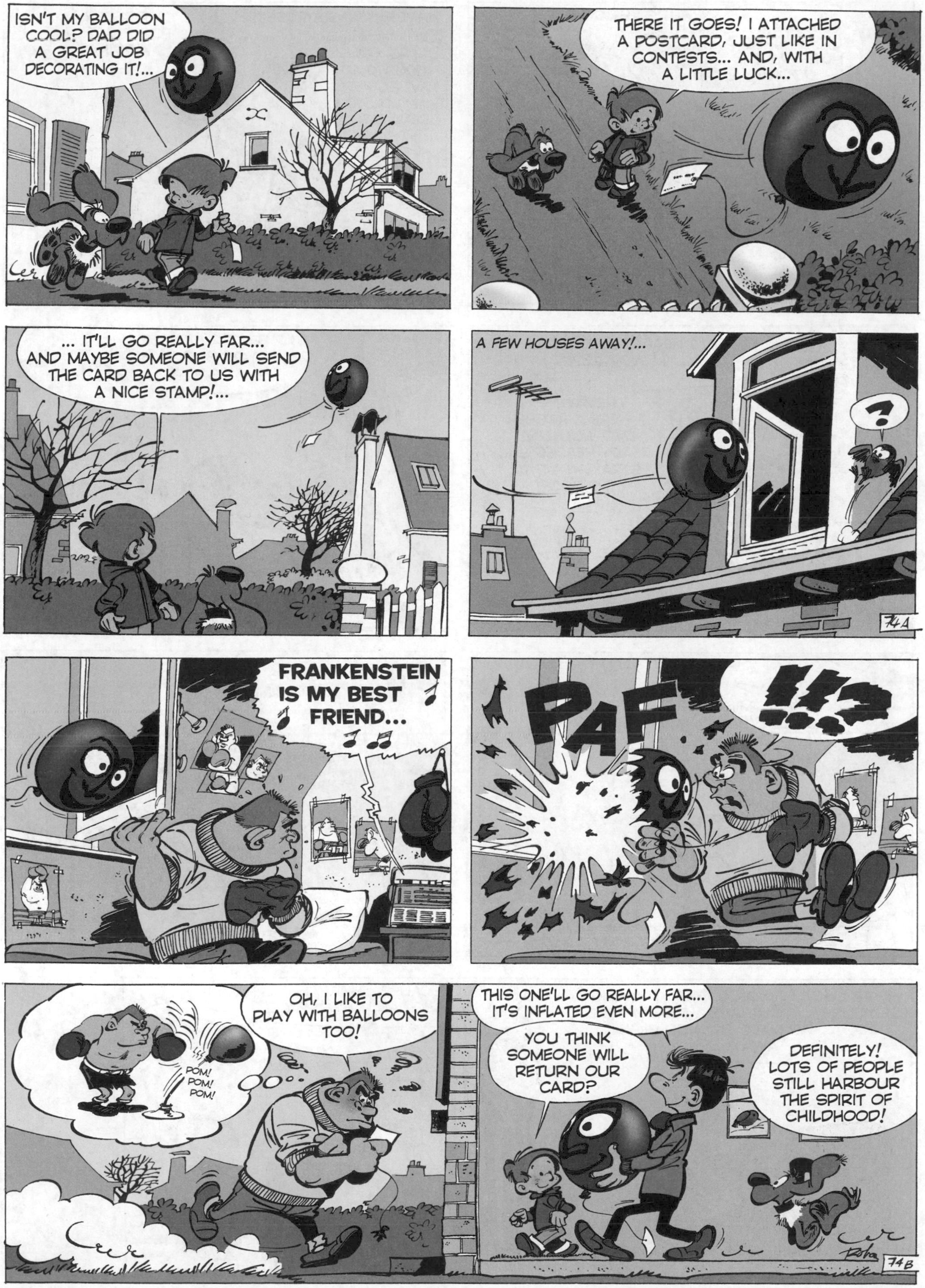

ISN'T MY BALLOON COOL? DAD DID A GREAT JOB DECORATING IT!...
THERE IT GOES! I ATTACHED A POSTCARD, JUST LIKE IN CONTESTS... AND, WITH A LITTLE LUCK...
... IT'LL GO REALLY FAR... AND MAYBE SOMEONE WILL SEND THE CARD BACK TO US WITH A NICE STAMP!...
A FEW HOUSES AWAY!...
?
FRANKENSTEIN IS MY BEST FRIEND...
PAF
!!?
POM! POM! POM!
OH, I LIKE TO PLAY WITH BALLOONS TOO!
THIS ONE'LL GO REALLY FAR... IT'S INFLATED EVEN MORE...
YOU THINK SOMEONE WILL RETURN OUR CARD?
DEFINITELY! LOTS OF PEOPLE STILL HARBOUR THE SPIRIT OF CHILDHOOD!

In the Company of Thieves

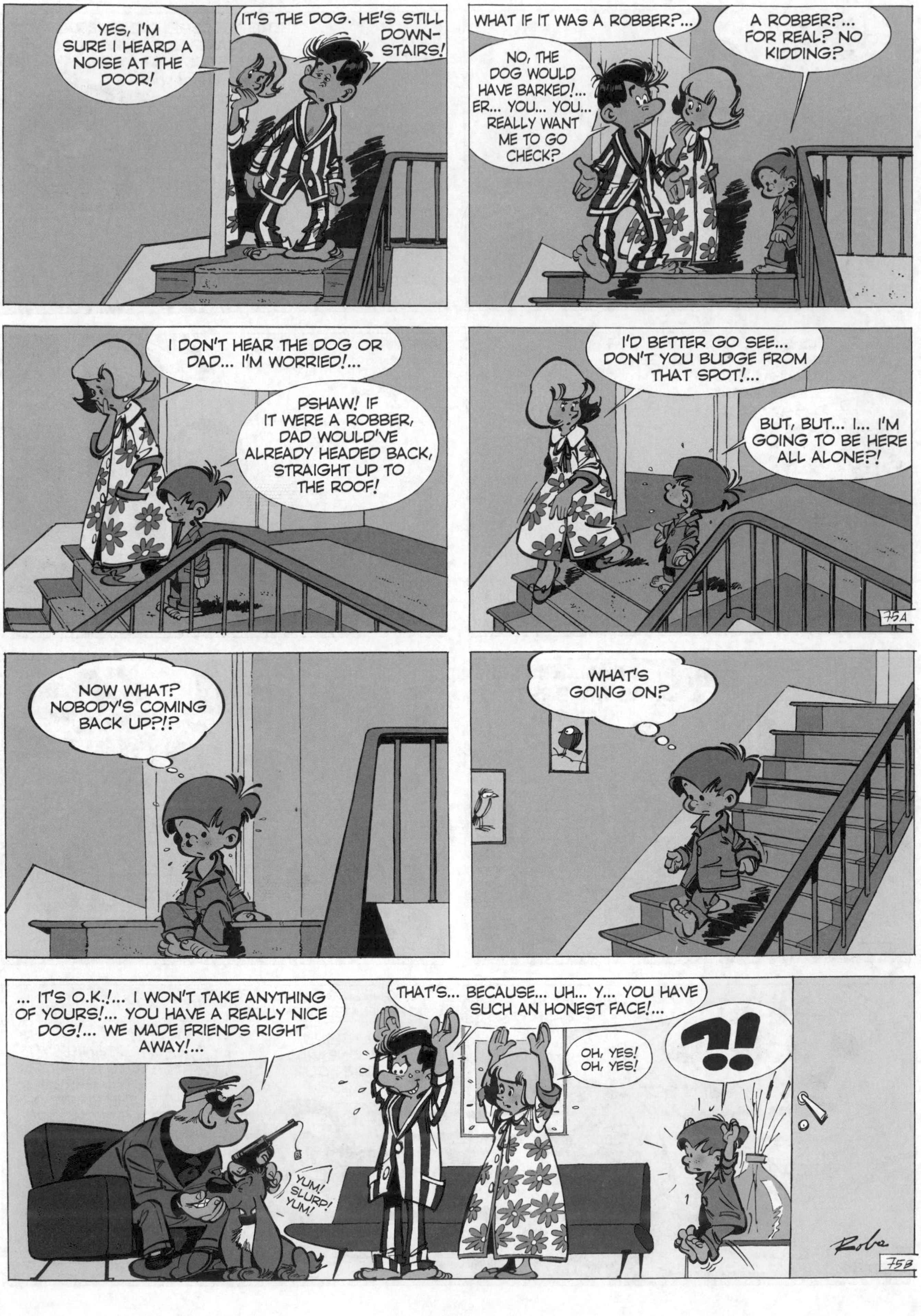
YES, I'M SURE I HEARD A NOISE AT THE DOOR!
IT'S THE DOG. HE'S STILL DOWN-STAIRS!
WHAT IF IT WAS A ROBBER?...
A ROBBER?... FOR REAL? NO KIDDING?
NO, THE DOG WOULD HAVE BARKED!... ER... YOU... YOU... REALLY WANT ME TO GO CHECK?
I DON'T HEAR THE DOG OR DAD... I'M WORRIED!...
PSHAW! IF IT WERE A ROBBER, DAD WOULD'VE ALREADY HEADED BACK, STRAIGHT UP TO THE ROOF!
I'D BETTER GO SEE... DON'T YOU BUDGE FROM THAT SPOT!...
BUT, BUT... I... I'M GOING TO BE HERE ALL ALONE?!
75A
NOW WHAT? NOBODY'S COMING BACK UP?!?
WHAT'S GOING ON?
... IT'S O.K.!... I WON'T TAKE ANYTHING OF YOURS!... YOU HAVE A REALLY NICE DOG!... WE MADE FRIENDS RIGHT AWAY!...
THAT'S... BECAUSE... UH... Y... YOU HAVE SUCH AN HONEST FACE!...
OH, YES! OH, YES!
?!
YUM! SLURP! YUM!
Roba
75B

The Taster

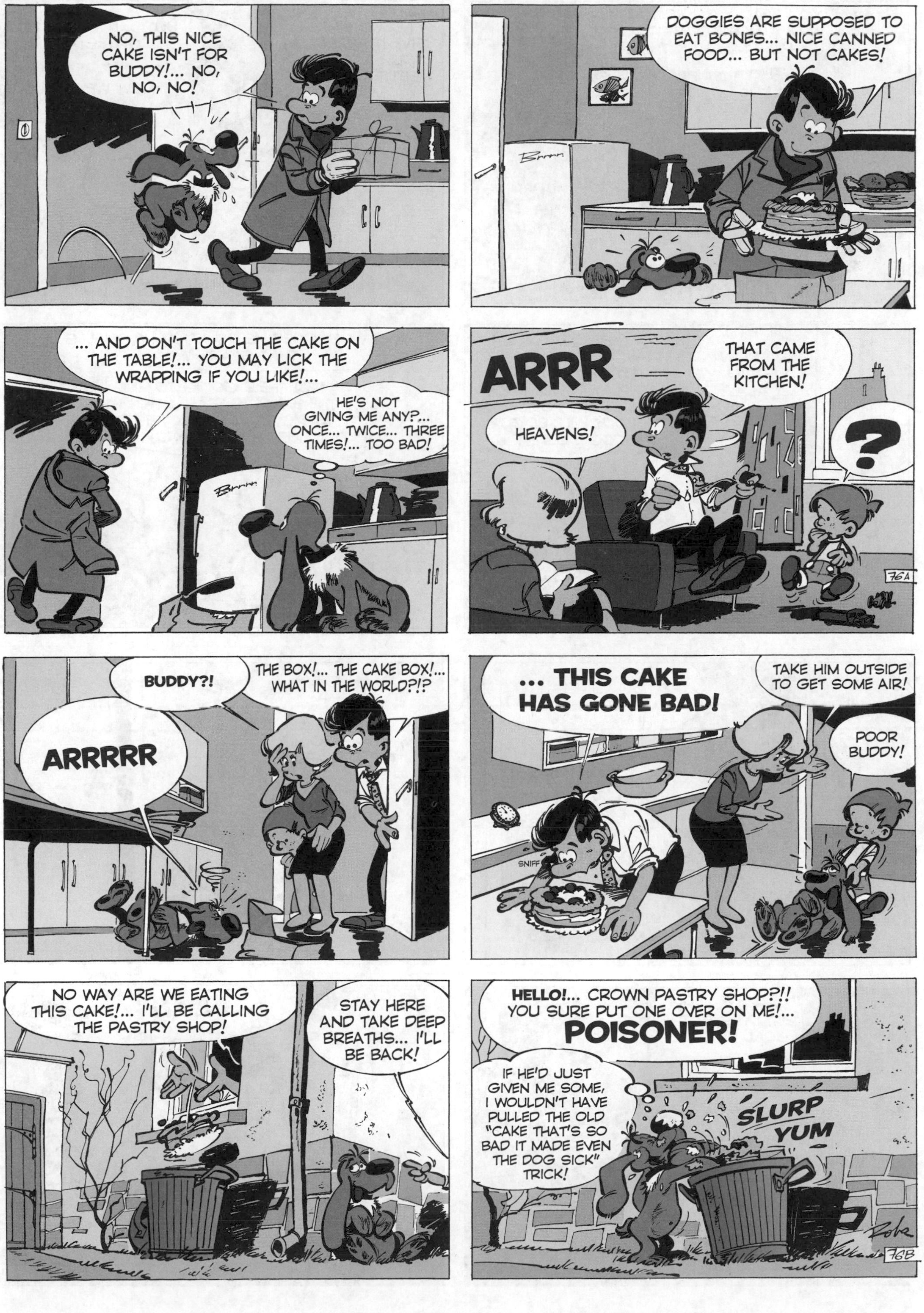
NO, THIS NICE CAKE ISN'T FOR BUDDY!... NO, NO, NO!
DOGGIES ARE SUPPOSED TO EAT BONES... NICE CANNED FOOD... BUT NOT CAKES!
... AND DON'T TOUCH THE CAKE ON THE TABLE!... YOU MAY LICK THE WRAPPING IF YOU LIKE!...
HE'S NOT GIVING ME ANY?... ONCE... TWICE... THREE TIMES!... TOO BAD!
ARRR
THAT CAME FROM THE KITCHEN!
HEAVENS!
?
BUDDY?!
THE BOX!... THE CAKE BOX!... WHAT IN THE WORLD?!?
ARRRRR
... THIS CAKE HAS GONE BAD!
TAKE HIM OUTSIDE TO GET SOME AIR!
POOR BUDDY!
SNIFF
NO WAY ARE WE EATING THIS CAKE!... I'LL BE CALLING THE PASTRY SHOP!
STAY HERE AND TAKE DEEP BREATHS... I'LL BE BACK!
HELLO!... CROWN PASTRY SHOP?!! YOU SURE PUT ONE OVER ON ME!... POISONER!
IF HE'D JUST GIVEN ME SOME, I WOULDN'T HAVE PULLED THE OLD "CAKE THAT'S SO BAD IT MADE EVEN THE DOG SICK" TRICK!
SLURP
YUM

The Blown Secret

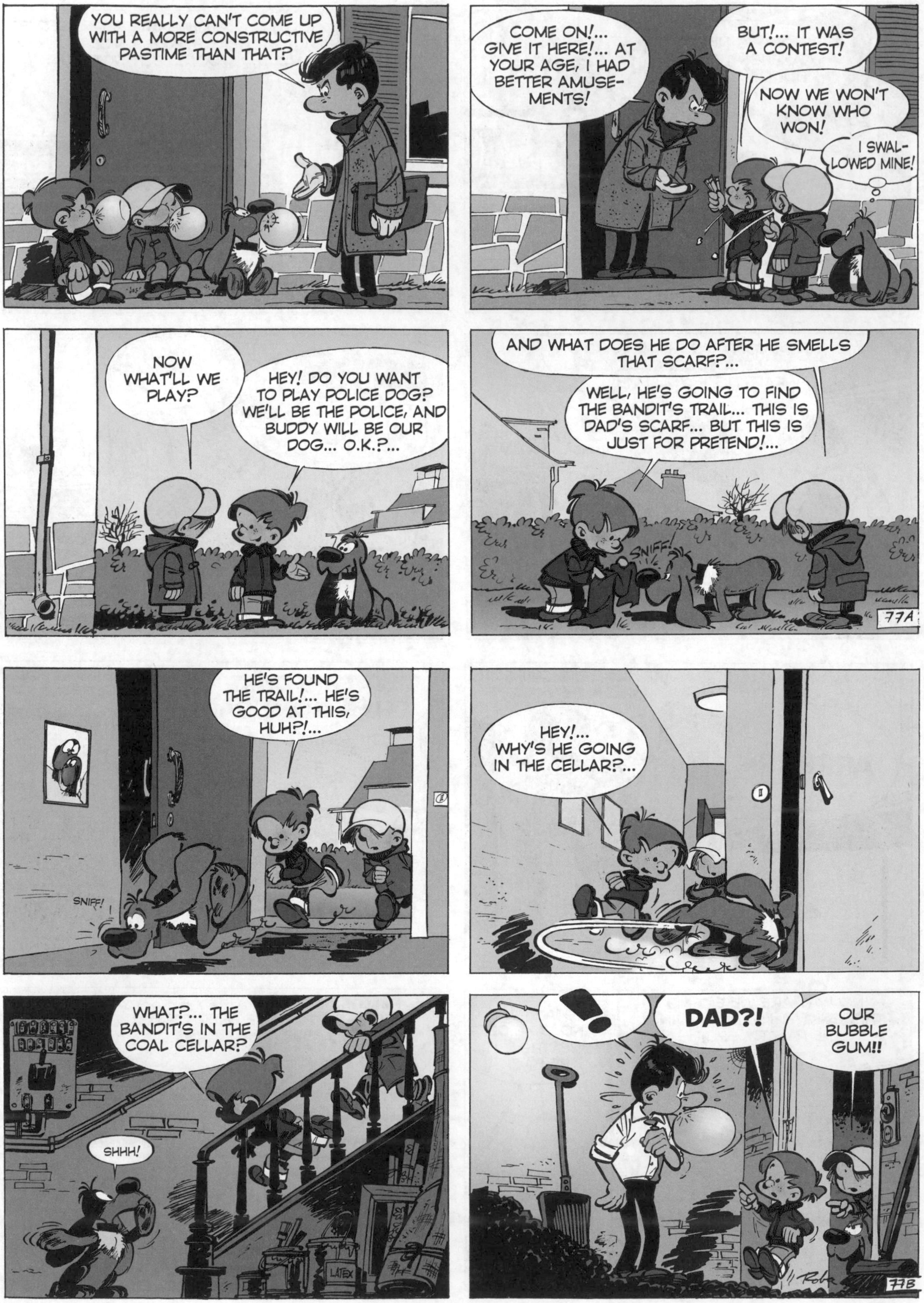

YOU REALLY CAN'T COME UP WITH A MORE CONSTRUCTIVE PASTIME THAN THAT?
COME ON!... GIVE IT HERE!... AT YOUR AGE, I HAD BETTER AMUSE-MENTS!
BUT!... IT WAS A CONTEST!
NOW WE WON'T KNOW WHO WON!
I SWAL-LOWED MINE!
NOW WHAT'LL WE PLAY?
HEY! DO YOU WANT TO PLAY POLICE DOG? WE'LL BE THE POLICE, AND BUDDY WILL BE OUR DOG... O.K.?...
AND WHAT DOES HE DO AFTER HE SMELLS THAT SCARF?...
WELL, HE'S GOING TO FIND THE BANDIT'S TRAIL... THIS IS DAD'S SCARF... BUT THIS IS JUST FOR PRETEND!...
SNIFF!
77A
HE'S FOUND THE TRAIL!... HE'S GOOD AT THIS, HUH?!...
SNIFF!
HEY!... WHY'S HE GOING IN THE CELLAR?...
WHAT?... THE BANDIT'S IN THE COAL CELLAR?
SHHH!
LATEX
!
DAD?!
OUR BUBBLE GUM!!
77B

The Art of Photography

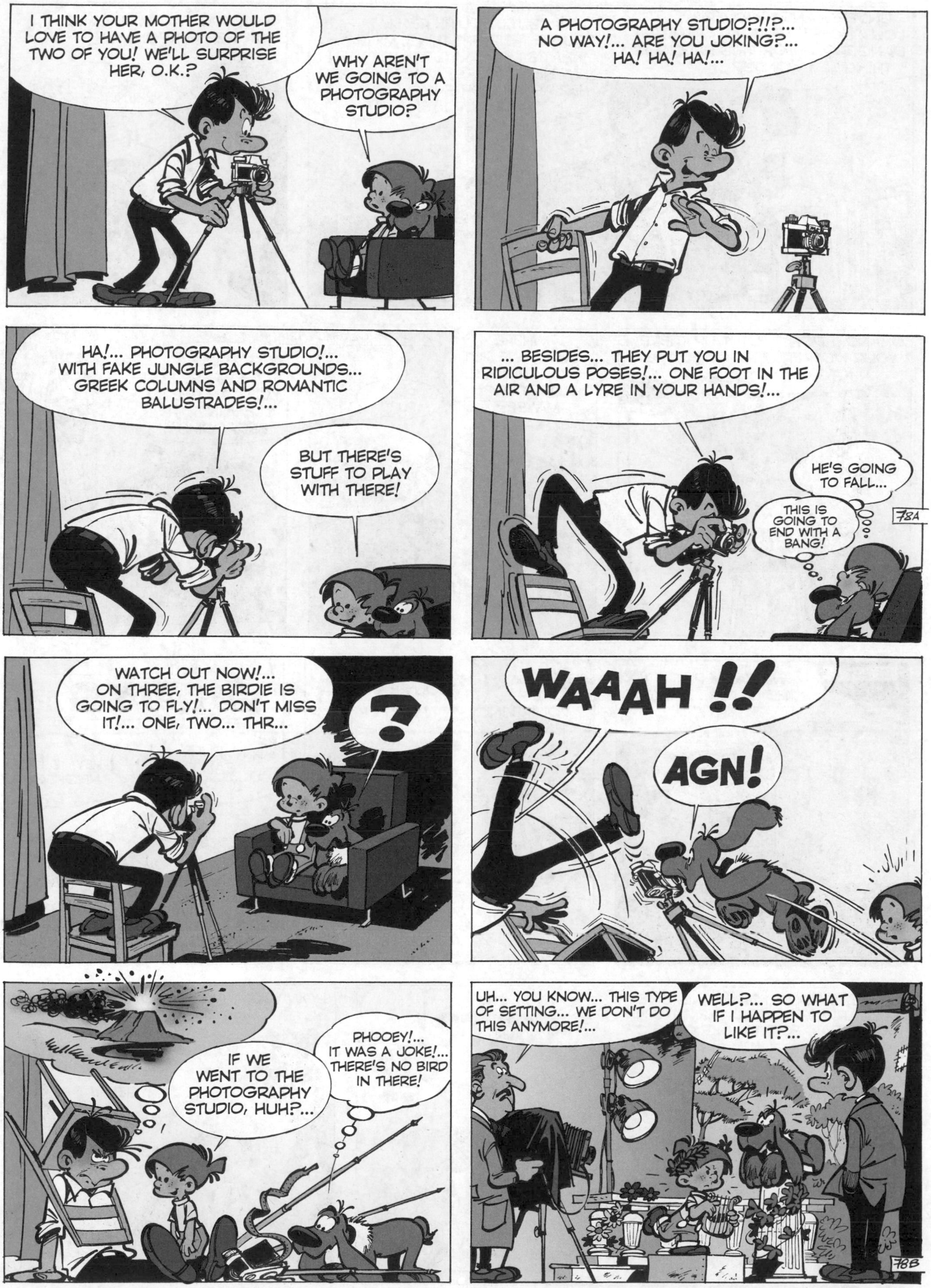
I THINK YOUR MOTHER WOULD LOVE TO HAVE A PHOTO OF THE TWO OF YOU! WE'LL SURPRISE HER, O.K.?
WHY AREN'T WE GOING TO A PHOTOGRAPHY STUDIO?
A PHOTOGRAPHY STUDIO?!!?... NO WAY!... ARE YOU JOKING?... HA! HA! HA!...
HA!... PHOTOGRAPHY STUDIO!... WITH FAKE JUNGLE BACKGROUNDS... GREEK COLUMNS AND ROMANTIC BALUSTRADES!...
BUT THERE'S STUFF TO PLAY WITH THERE!
... BESIDES... THEY PUT YOU IN RIDICULOUS POSES!... ONE FOOT IN THE AIR AND A LYRE IN YOUR HANDS!...
HE'S GOING TO FALL...
THIS IS GOING TO END WITH A BANG!
78A
WATCH OUT NOW!... ON THREE, THE BIRDIE IS GOING TO FLY!... DON'T MISS IT!... ONE, TWO... THR...
?
WAAAH !!
AGN!
IF WE WENT TO THE PHOTOGRAPHY STUDIO, HUH?...
PHOOEY!... IT WAS A JOKE!... THERE'S NO BIRD IN THERE!
UH... YOU KNOW... THIS TYPE OF SETTING... WE DON'T DO THIS ANYMORE!...
WELL?... SO WHAT IF I HAPPEN TO LIKE IT?...
78B

Consummate Hosts

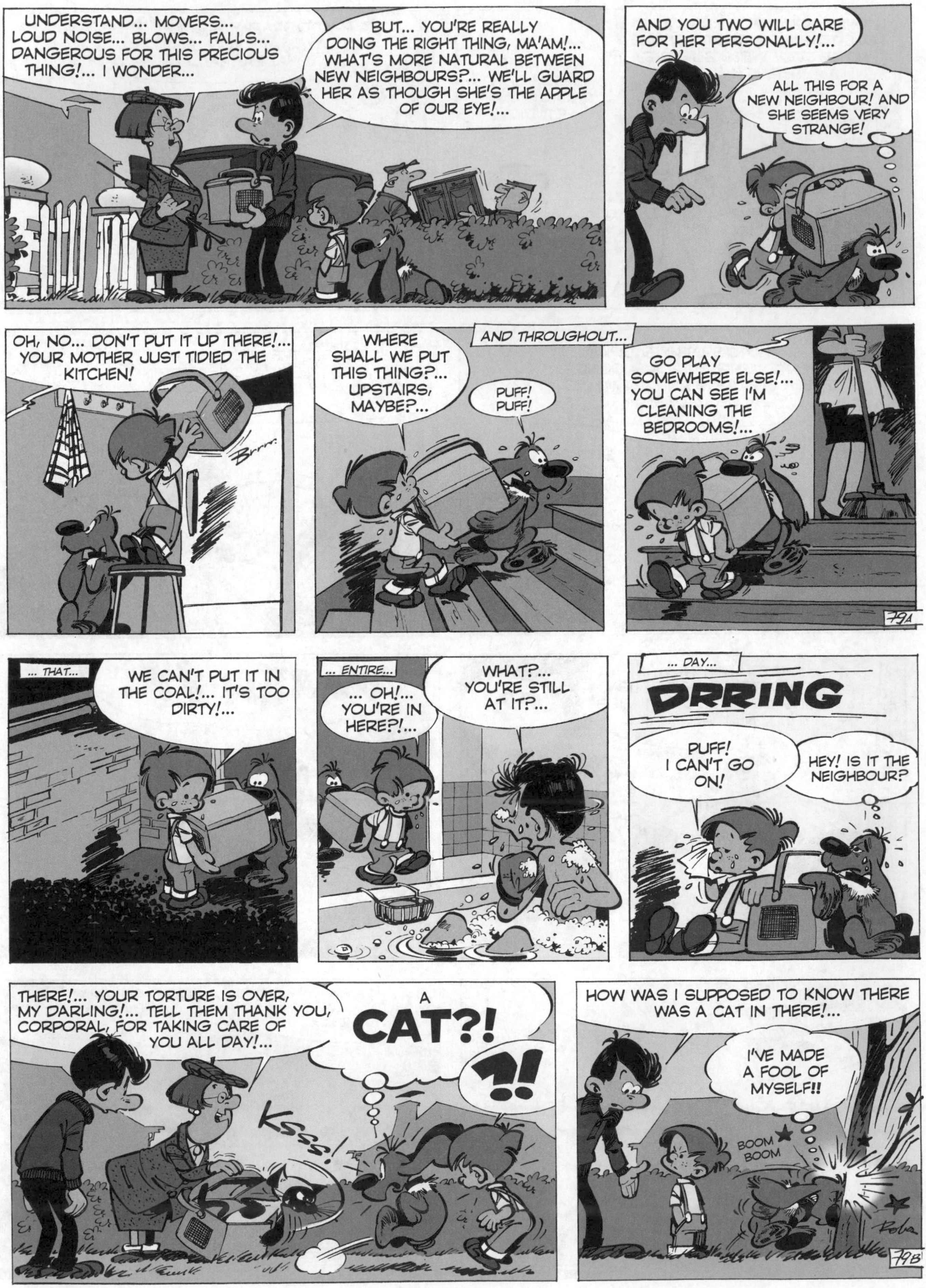
UNDERSTAND... MOVERS... LOUD NOISE... BLOWS... FALLS... DANGEROUS FOR THIS PRECIOUS THING!... I WONDER...
BUT... YOU'RE REALLY DOING THE RIGHT THING, MA'AM!... WHAT'S MORE NATURAL BETWEEN NEW NEIGHBOURS?... WE'LL GUARD HER AS THOUGH SHE'S THE APPLE OF OUR EYE!...
AND YOU TWO WILL CARE FOR HER PERSONALLY!...
ALL THIS FOR A NEW NEIGHBOUR! AND SHE SEEMS VERY STRANGE!
OH, NO... DON'T PUT IT UP THERE!... YOUR MOTHER JUST TIDIED THE KITCHEN!
Brrr
AND THROUGHOUT...
WHERE SHALL WE PUT THIS THING?... UPSTAIRS, MAYBE?...
PUFF! PUFF!
GO PLAY SOMEWHERE ELSE!... YOU CAN SEE I'M CLEANING THE BEDROOMS!...
79A
... THAT...
WE CAN'T PUT IT IN THE COAL!... IT'S TOO DIRTY!...
... ENTIRE...
... OH!... YOU'RE IN HERE?!...
WHAT?... YOU'RE STILL AT IT?...
... DAY...
DRRING
PUFF! I CAN'T GO ON!
HEY! IS IT THE NEIGHBOUR?
THERE!... YOUR TORTURE IS OVER, MY DARLING!... TELL THEM THANK YOU, CORPORAL, FOR TAKING CARE OF YOU ALL DAY!...
A CAT?!
KSSS!
?!
HOW WAS I SUPPOSED TO KNOW THERE WAS A CAT IN THERE!...
I'VE MADE A FOOL OF MYSELF!!
BOOM BOOM
Roba
79B

Porter!

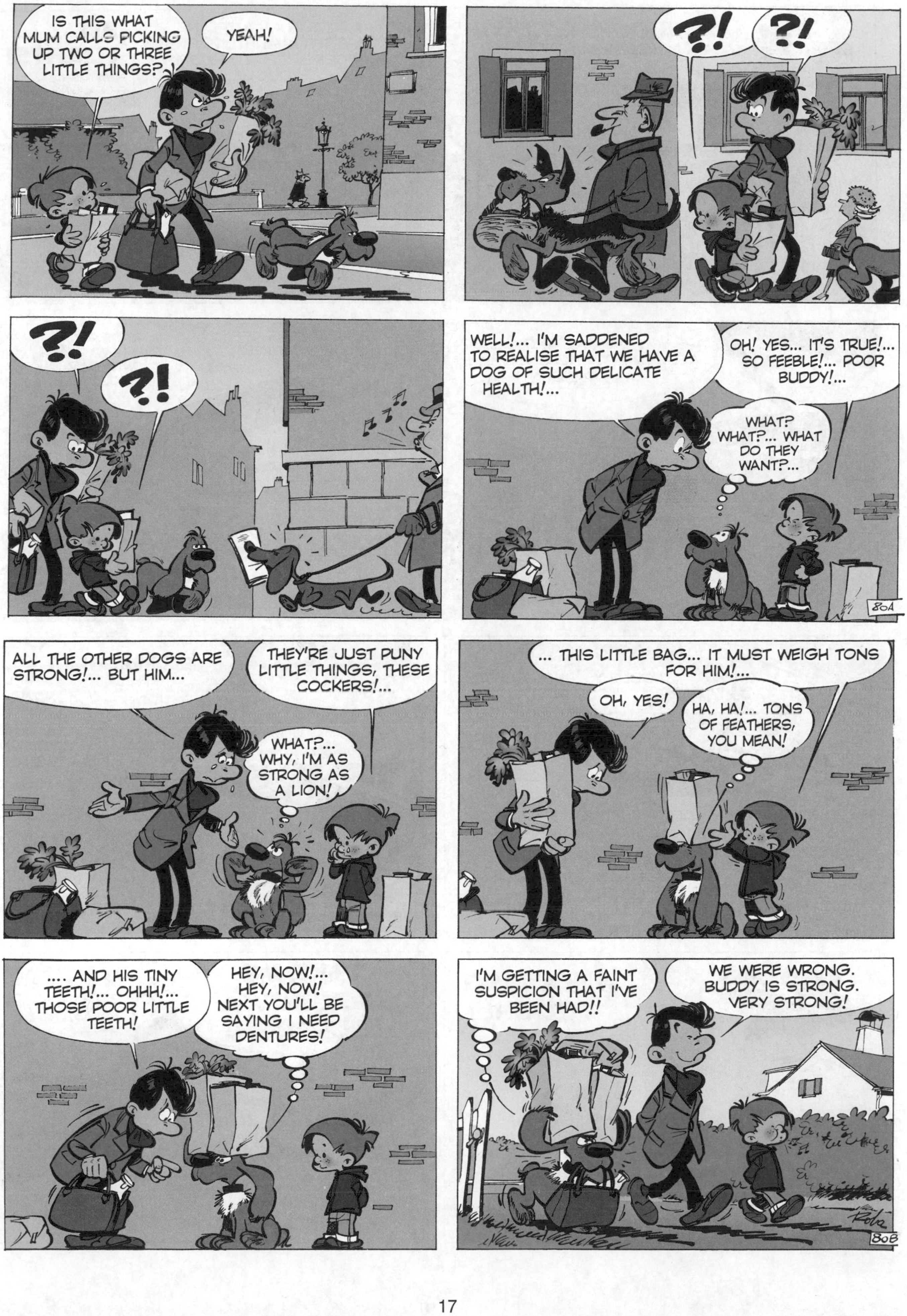

IS THIS WHAT MUM CALLS PICKING UP TWO OR THREE LITTLE THINGS?
YEAH!
?!
?!
?!
?!
WELL!... I'M SADDENED TO REALISE THAT WE HAVE A DOG OF SUCH DELICATE HEALTH!...
OH! YES... IT'S TRUE!... SO FEEBLE!... POOR BUDDY!...
WHAT? WHAT?... WHAT DO THEY WANT?...
80A
ALL THE OTHER DOGS ARE STRONG!... BUT HIM...
THEY'RE JUST PUNY LITTLE THINGS, THESE COCKERS!...
WHAT?... WHY, I'M AS STRONG AS A LION!
... THIS LITTLE BAG... IT MUST WEIGH TONS FOR HIM!...
OH, YES!
HA, HA!... TONS OF FEATHERS, YOU MEAN!
.... AND HIS TINY TEETH!... OHHH!... THOSE POOR LITTLE TEETH!
HEY, NOW!... HEY, NOW! NEXT YOU'LL BE SAYING I NEED DENTURES!
I'M GETTING A FAINT SUSPICION THAT I'VE BEEN HAD!!
WE WERE WRONG. BUDDY IS STRONG. VERY STRONG!
Roba
80B

Medical Flight

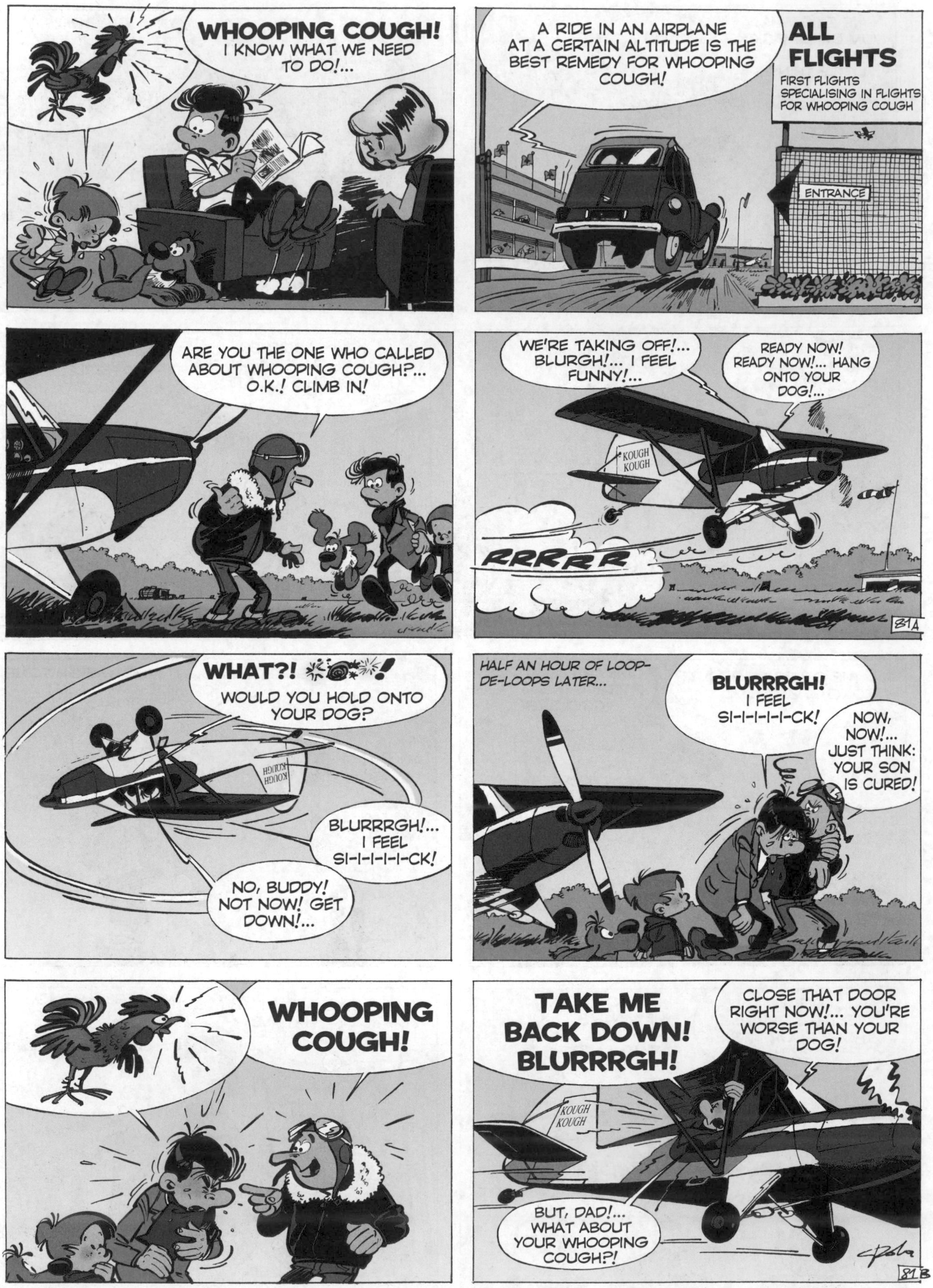

WHOOPING COUGH! I KNOW WHAT WE NEED TO DO!...
A RIDE IN AN AIRPLANE AT A CERTAIN ALTITUDE IS THE BEST REMEDY FOR WHOOPING COUGH!
ALL FLIGHTS
FIRST FLIGHTS SPECIALISING IN FLIGHTS FOR WHOOPING COUGH
ENTRANCE
ARE YOU THE ONE WHO CALLED ABOUT WHOOPING COUGH?... O.K.! CLIMB IN!
WE'RE TAKING OFF!... BLURGH!... I FEEL FUNNY!...
READY NOW! READY NOW!... HANG ONTO YOUR DOG!...
KOUGH KOUGH
RRRRR
81A
WHAT?!
WOULD YOU HOLD ONTO YOUR DOG?
BLURRRGH!... I FEEL SI-I-I-I-I-CK!
NO, BUDDY! NOT NOW! GET DOWN!...
HALF AN HOUR OF LOOP-DE-LOOPS LATER...
BLURRRGH! I FEEL SI-I-I-I-I-CK!
NOW, NOW!... JUST THINK: YOUR SON IS CURED!
WHOOPING COUGH!
TAKE ME BACK DOWN! BLURRRGH!
CLOSE THAT DOOR RIGHT NOW!... YOU'RE WORSE THAN YOUR DOG!
KOUGH KOUGH
BUT, DAD!... WHAT ABOUT YOUR WHOOPING COUGH?!
81B

Aerial Demonstration

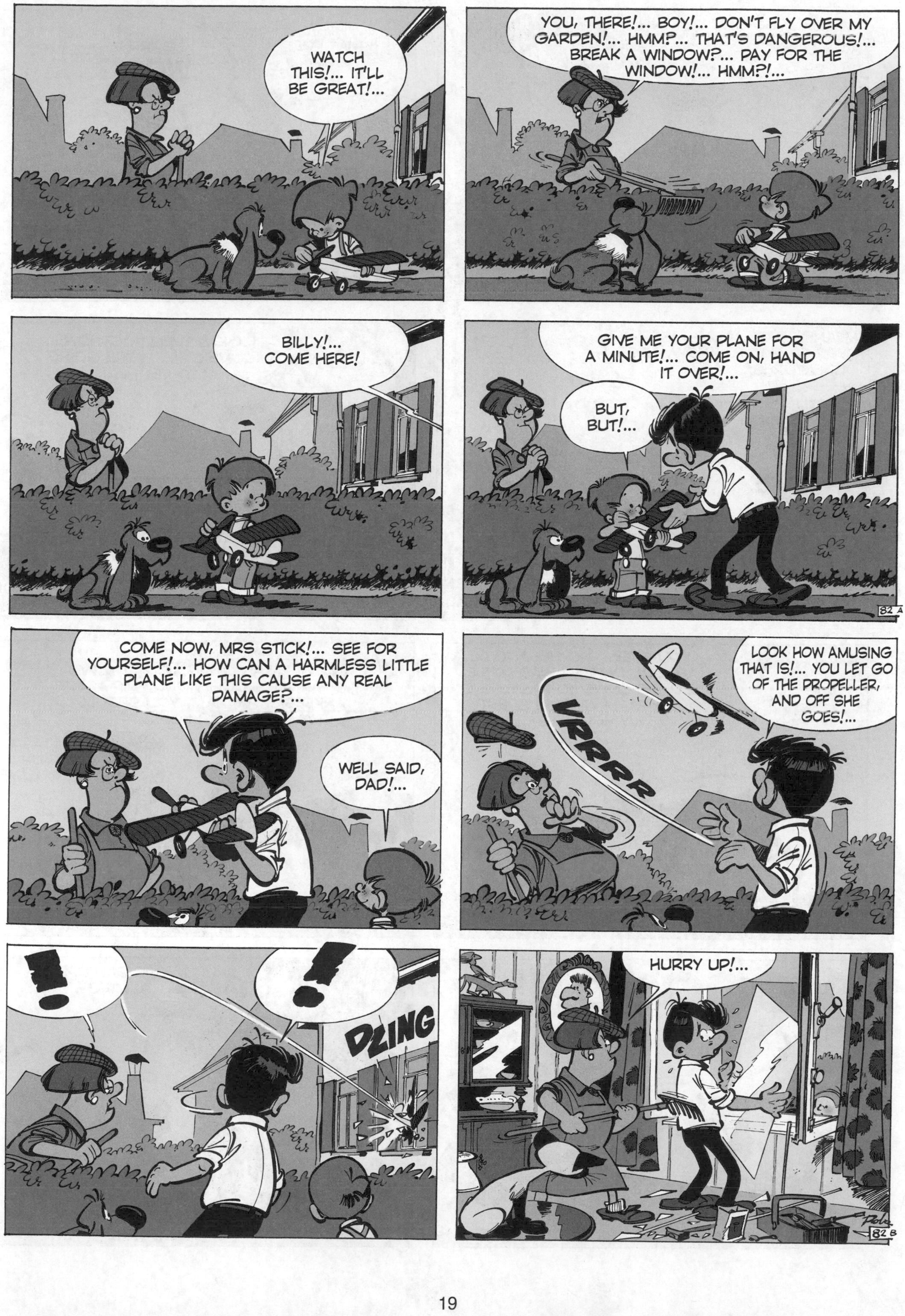

WATCH THIS!... IT'LL BE GREAT!...
YOU, THERE!... BOY!... DON'T FLY OVER MY GARDEN!... HMM?... THAT'S DANGEROUS!... BREAK A WINDOW?... PAY FOR THE WINDOW!... HMM?!...
BILLY!... COME HERE!
GIVE ME YOUR PLANE FOR A MINUTE!... COME ON, HAND IT OVER!...
BUT, BUT!...
82 A
COME NOW, MRS STICK!... SEE FOR YOURSELF!... HOW CAN A HARMLESS LITTLE PLANE LIKE THIS CAUSE ANY REAL DAMAGE?...
WELL SAID, DAD!...
LOOK HOW AMUSING THAT IS!... YOU LET GO OF THE PROPELLER, AND OFF SHE GOES!...
VRRRRR
!
!
DZING
HURRY UP!...
82 B

Farm Memories

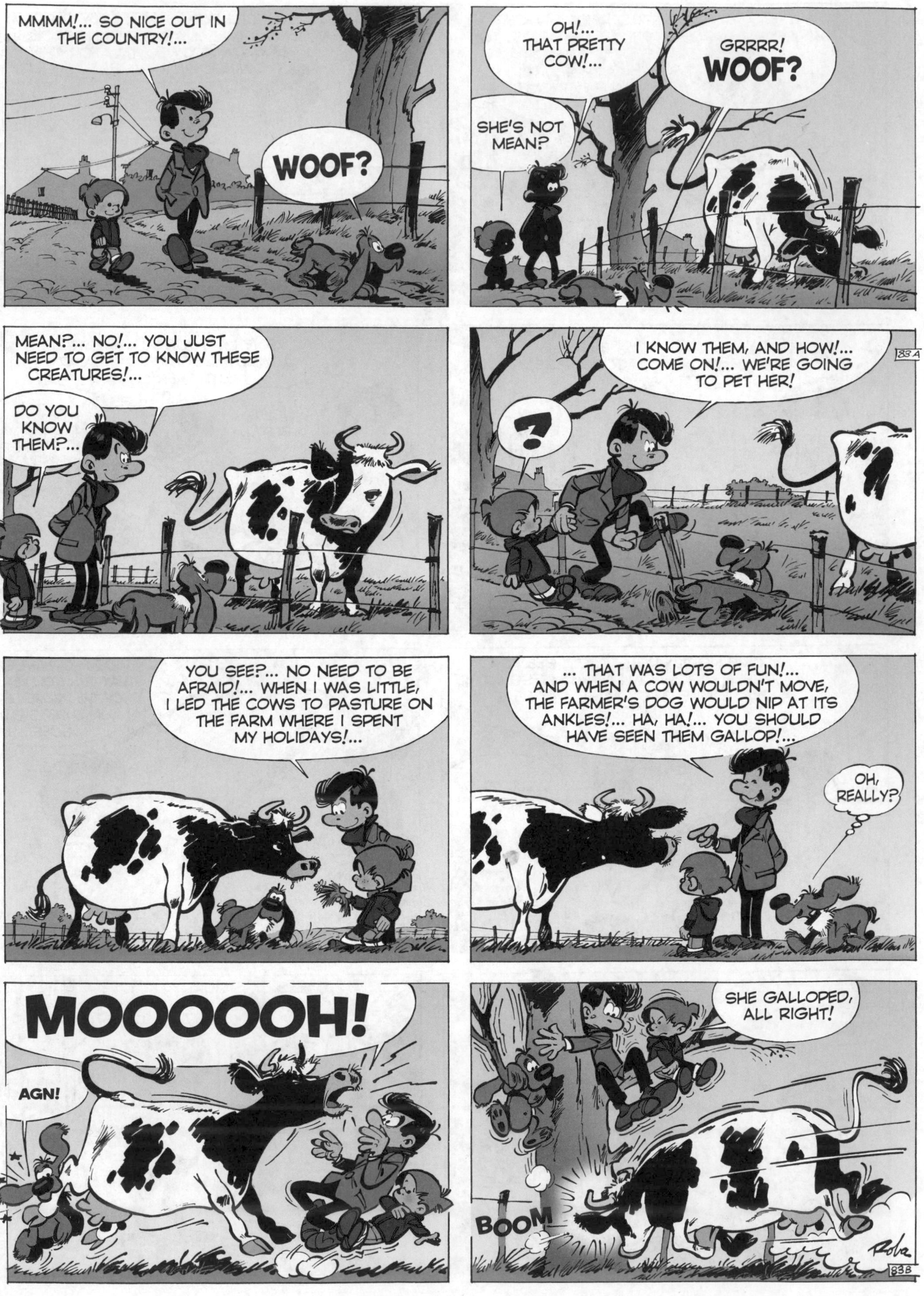

MMMM!... SO NICE OUT IN THE COUNTRY!...
WOOF?
OH!... THAT PRETTY COW!...
SHE'S NOT MEAN?
GRRRR! WOOF?
MEAN?... NO!... YOU JUST NEED TO GET TO KNOW THESE CREATURES!...
DO YOU KNOW THEM?...
?
I KNOW THEM, AND HOW!... COME ON!... WE'RE GOING TO PET HER!
83 A
YOU SEE?... NO NEED TO BE AFRAID!... WHEN I WAS LITTLE, I LED THE COWS TO PASTURE ON THE FARM WHERE I SPENT MY HOLIDAYS!...
... THAT WAS LOTS OF FUN!... AND WHEN A COW WOULDN'T MOVE, THE FARMER'S DOG WOULD NIP AT ITS ANKLES!... HA, HA!... YOU SHOULD HAVE SEEN THEM GALLOP!...
OH, REALLY?
MOOOOOH!
AGN!
SHE GALLOPED, ALL RIGHT!
BOOM
Roba
83B

Home Delivery

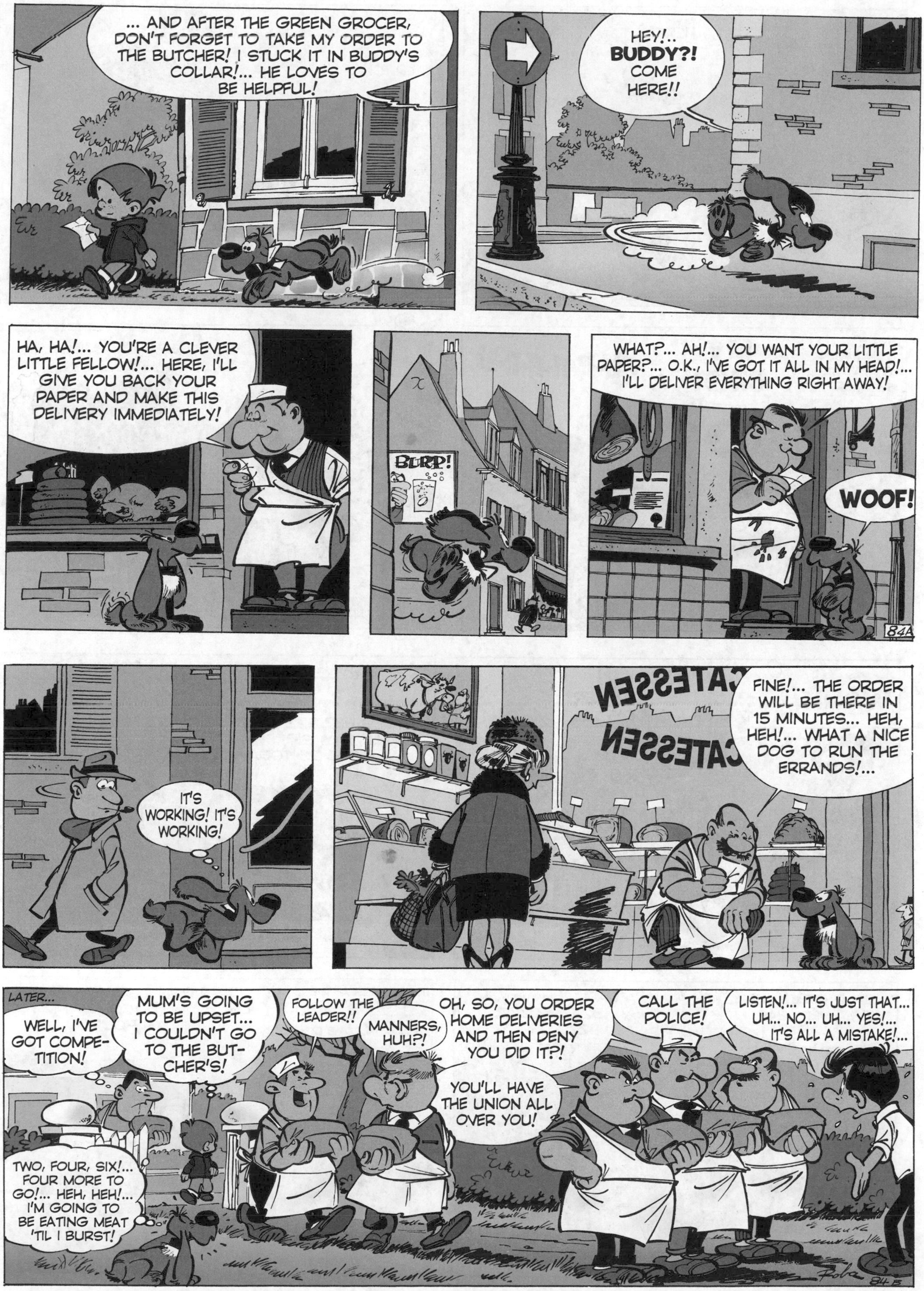

... AND AFTER THE GREEN GROCER, DON'T FORGET TO TAKE MY ORDER TO THE BUTCHER! I STUCK IT IN BUDDY'S COLLAR!... HE LOVES TO BE HELPFUL!
HEY!.. **BUDDY?!** COME HERE!!
HA, HA!... YOU'RE A CLEVER LITTLE FELLOW!... HERE, I'LL GIVE YOU BACK YOUR PAPER AND MAKE THIS DELIVERY IMMEDIATELY!
BURP!
WHAT?... AH!... YOU WANT YOUR LITTLE PAPER?... O.K., I'VE GOT IT ALL IN MY HEAD!... I'LL DELIVER EVERYTHING RIGHT AWAY!
WOOF!
IT'S WORKING! IT'S WORKING!
CATESSEN
FINE!... THE ORDER WILL BE THERE IN 15 MINUTES... HEH, HEH!... WHAT A NICE DOG TO RUN THE ERRANDS!...
LATER...
WELL, I'VE GOT COMPE-TITION!
MUM'S GOING TO BE UPSET... I COULDN'T GO TO THE BUT-CHER'S!
FOLLOW THE LEADER!!
MANNERS, HUH?!
OH, SO, YOU ORDER HOME DELIVERIES AND THEN DENY YOU DID IT?!
YOU'LL HAVE THE UNION ALL OVER YOU!
CALL THE POLICE!
LISTEN!... IT'S JUST THAT... UH... NO... UH... YES!... IT'S ALL A MISTAKE!...
TWO, FOUR, SIX!... FOUR MORE TO GO!... HEH, HEH!... I'M GOING TO BE EATING MEAT 'TIL I BURST!

Dog on Wheels

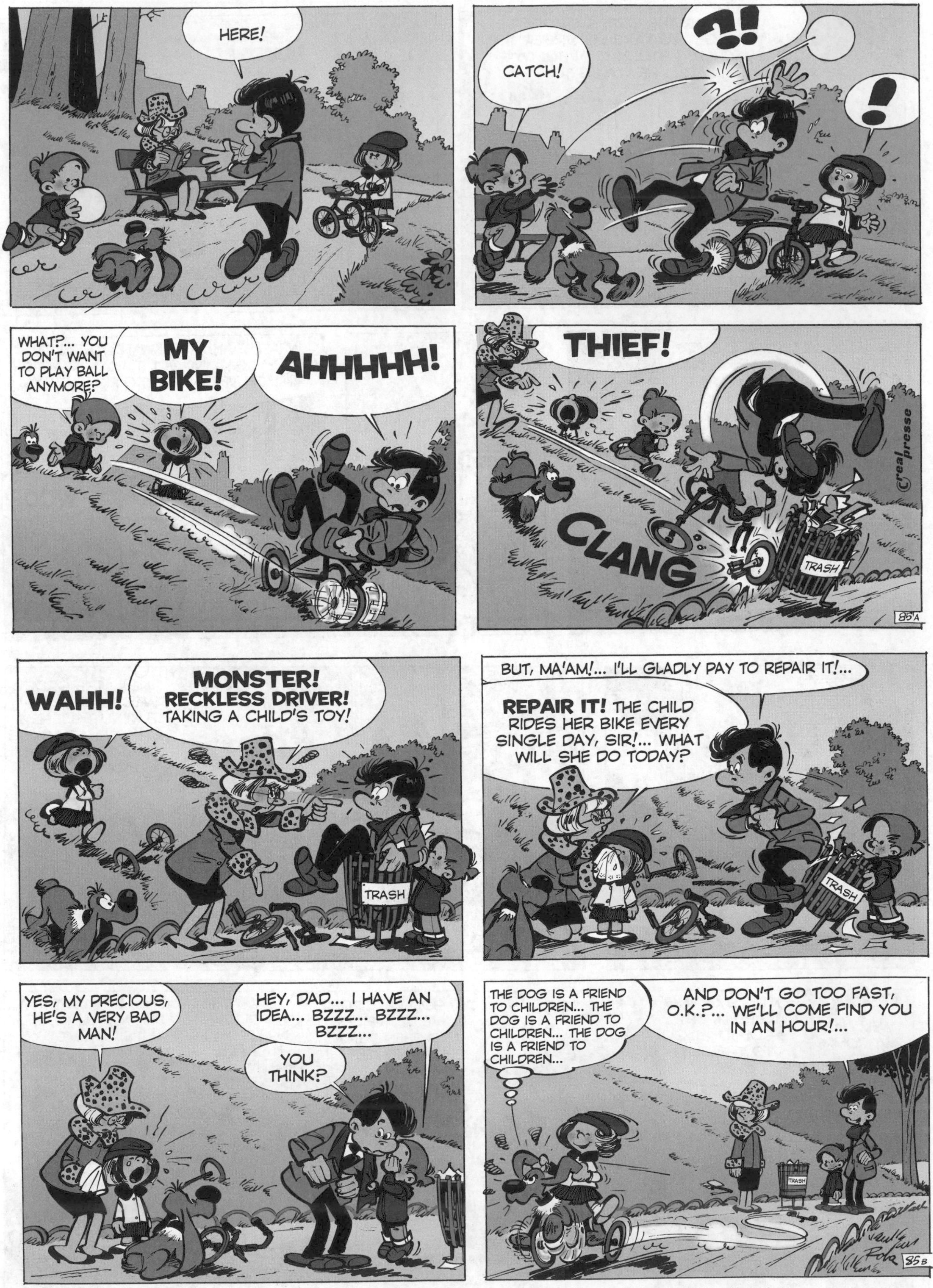
HERE!
CATCH!
?!
!
WHAT?... YOU DON'T WANT TO PLAY BALL ANYMORE?
MY BIKE!
AHHHHH!
THIEF!
CLANG
TRASH
©real presse
85A
WAHH!
MONSTER! RECKLESS DRIVER! TAKING A CHILD'S TOY!
TRASH
BUT, MA'AM!... I'LL GLADLY PAY TO REPAIR IT!...
REPAIR IT! THE CHILD RIDES HER BIKE EVERY SINGLE DAY, SIR!... WHAT WILL SHE DO TODAY?
TRASH
YES, MY PRECIOUS, HE'S A VERY BAD MAN!
HEY, DAD... I HAVE AN IDEA... BZZZ... BZZZ... BZZZ...
YOU THINK?
THE DOG IS A FRIEND TO CHILDREN... THE DOG IS A FRIEND TO CHILDREN... THE DOG IS A FRIEND TO CHILDREN...
AND DON'T GO TOO FAST, O.K.?... WE'LL COME FIND YOU IN AN HOUR!...
TRASH
Roba
85B

Eggheads!

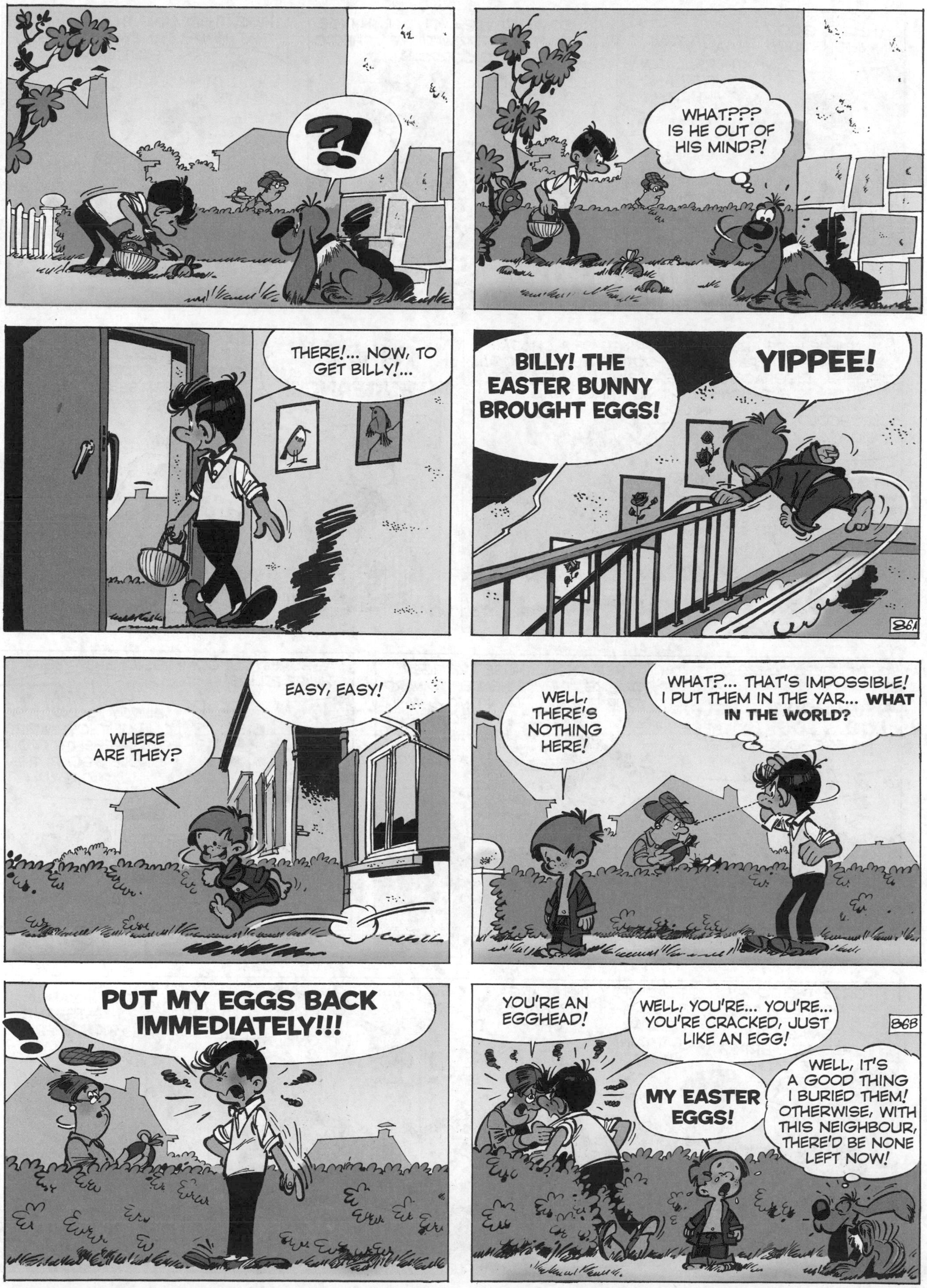
?!
WHAT??? IS HE OUT OF HIS MIND?!
THERE!... NOW, TO GET BILLY!...
BILLY! THE EASTER BUNNY BROUGHT EGGS!
YIPPEE!
86A
WHERE ARE THEY?
EASY, EASY!
WELL, THERE'S NOTHING HERE!
WHAT?... THAT'S IMPOSSIBLE! I PUT THEM IN THE YAR... WHAT IN THE WORLD?
!
PUT MY EGGS BACK IMMEDIATELY!!!
YOU'RE AN EGGHEAD!
WELL, YOU'RE... YOU'RE... YOU'RE CRACKED, JUST LIKE AN EGG!
86B
MY EASTER EGGS!
WELL, IT'S A GOOD THING I BURIED THEM! OTHERWISE, WITH THIS NEIGHBOUR, THERE'D BE NONE LEFT NOW!

The Beast Has Been Released

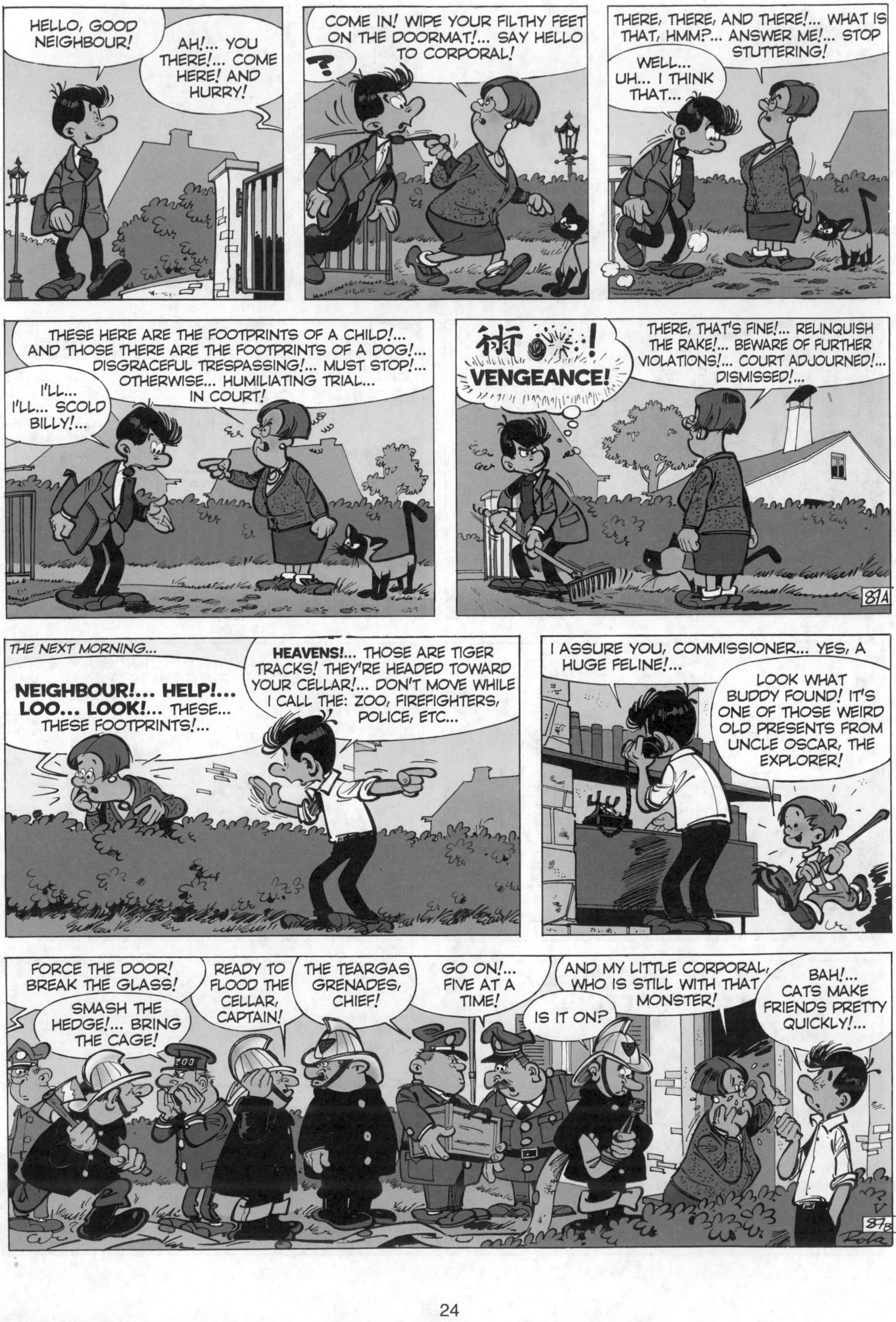

HELLO, GOOD NEIGHBOUR!
AH!... YOU THERE!... COME HERE! AND HURRY!
COME IN! WIPE YOUR FILTHY FEET ON THE DOORMAT!... SAY HELLO TO CORPORAL!
?
THERE, THERE, AND THERE!... WHAT IS THAT, HMM?... ANSWER ME!... STOP STUTTERING!
WELL... UH... I THINK THAT...
THESE HERE ARE THE FOOTPRINTS OF A CHILD!... AND THOSE THERE ARE THE FOOTPRINTS OF A DOG!... DISGRACEFUL TRESPASSING!... MUST STOP!... OTHERWISE... HUMILIATING TRIAL... IN COURT!
I'LL... I'LL... SCOLD BILLY!...
VENGEANCE!
THERE, THAT'S FINE!... RELINQUISH THE RAKE!... BEWARE OF FURTHER VIOLATIONS!... COURT ADJOURNED!... DISMISSED!...
THE NEXT MORNING...
NEIGHBOUR!... HELP!... LOO... LOOK!... THESE... THESE FOOTPRINTS!...
HEAVENS!... THOSE ARE TIGER TRACKS! THEY'RE HEADED TOWARD YOUR CELLAR!... DON'T MOVE WHILE I CALL THE: ZOO, FIREFIGHTERS, POLICE, ETC...
I ASSURE YOU, COMMISSIONER... YES, A HUGE FELINE!...
LOOK WHAT BUDDY FOUND! IT'S ONE OF THOSE WEIRD OLD PRESENTS FROM UNCLE OSCAR, THE EXPLORER!
FORCE THE DOOR! BREAK THE GLASS!
SMASH THE HEDGE!... BRING THE CAGE!
READY TO FLOOD THE CELLAR, CAPTAIN!
THE TEARGAS GRENADES, CHIEF!
GO ON!... FIVE AT A TIME!
IS IT ON?
AND MY LITTLE CORPORAL, WHO IS STILL WITH THAT MONSTER!
BAH!... CATS MAKE FRIENDS PRETTY QUICKLY!...
ZOO

Barbecued Water

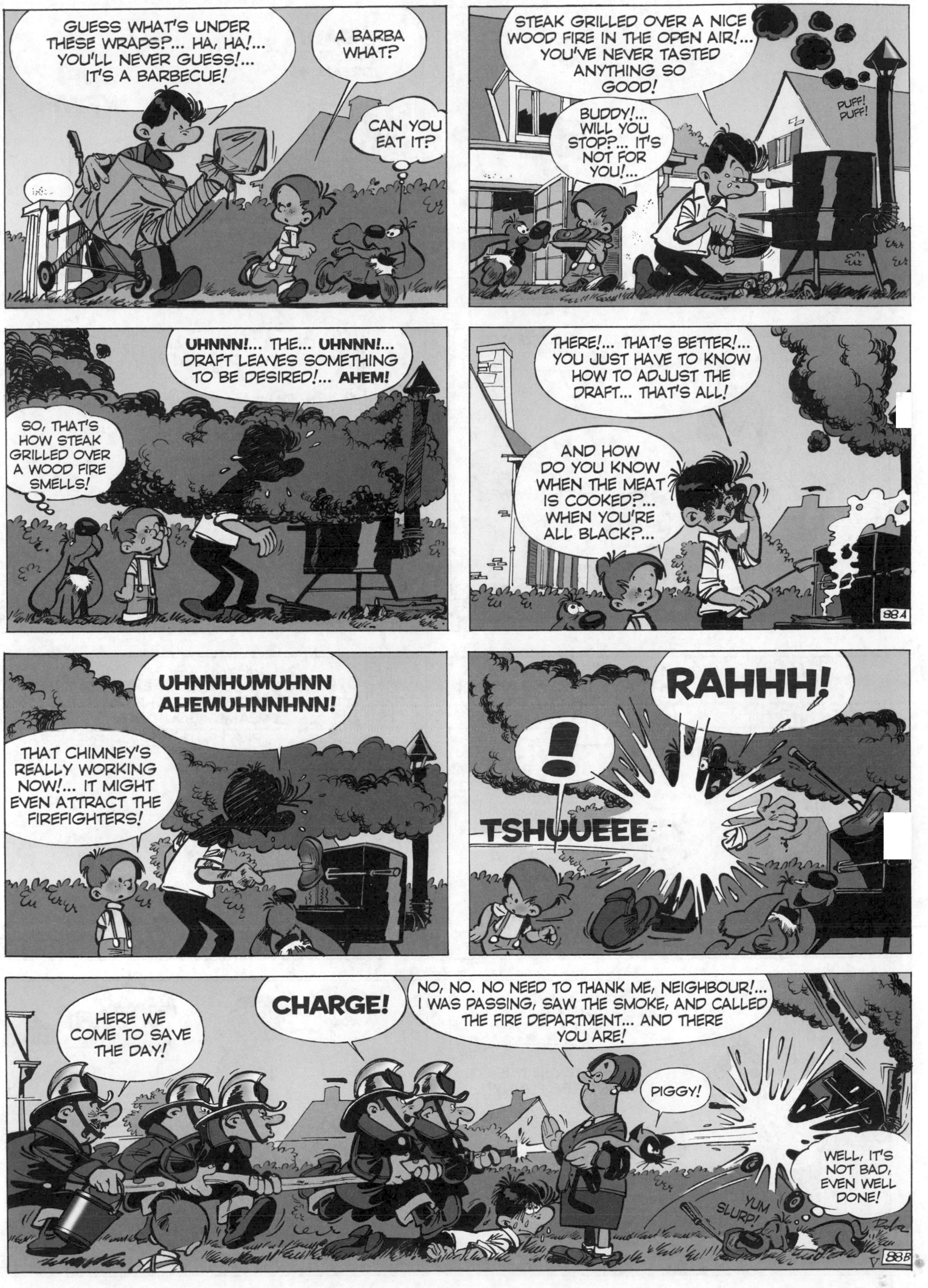

GUESS WHAT'S UNDER THESE WRAPS?... HA, HA!... YOU'LL NEVER GUESS!... IT'S A BARBECUE!
A BARBA WHAT?
CAN YOU EAT IT?
STEAK GRILLED OVER A NICE WOOD FIRE IN THE OPEN AIR!... YOU'VE NEVER TASTED ANYTHING SO GOOD!
BUDDY!... WILL YOU STOP?... IT'S NOT FOR YOU!...
PUFF! PUFF!
UHNNN!... THE... UHNNN!... DRAFT LEAVES SOMETHING TO BE DESIRED!... AHEM!
SO, THAT'S HOW STEAK GRILLED OVER A WOOD FIRE SMELLS!
THERE!... THAT'S BETTER!... YOU JUST HAVE TO KNOW HOW TO ADJUST THE DRAFT... THAT'S ALL!
AND HOW DO YOU KNOW WHEN THE MEAT IS COOKED?... WHEN YOU'RE ALL BLACK?...
88 A
UHNNHUMUHNN AHEMUHNNHNN!
THAT CHIMNEY'S REALLY WORKING NOW!... IT MIGHT EVEN ATTRACT THE FIREFIGHTERS!
RAHHH!
!
TSHUUEEE
HERE WE COME TO SAVE THE DAY!
CHARGE!
NO, NO. NO NEED TO THANK ME, NEIGHBOUR!... I WAS PASSING, SAW THE SMOKE, AND CALLED THE FIRE DEPARTMENT... AND THERE YOU ARE!
PIGGY!
WELL, IT'S NOT BAD, EVEN WELL DONE!
YUM SLURP!
88 B

Funny Dream!

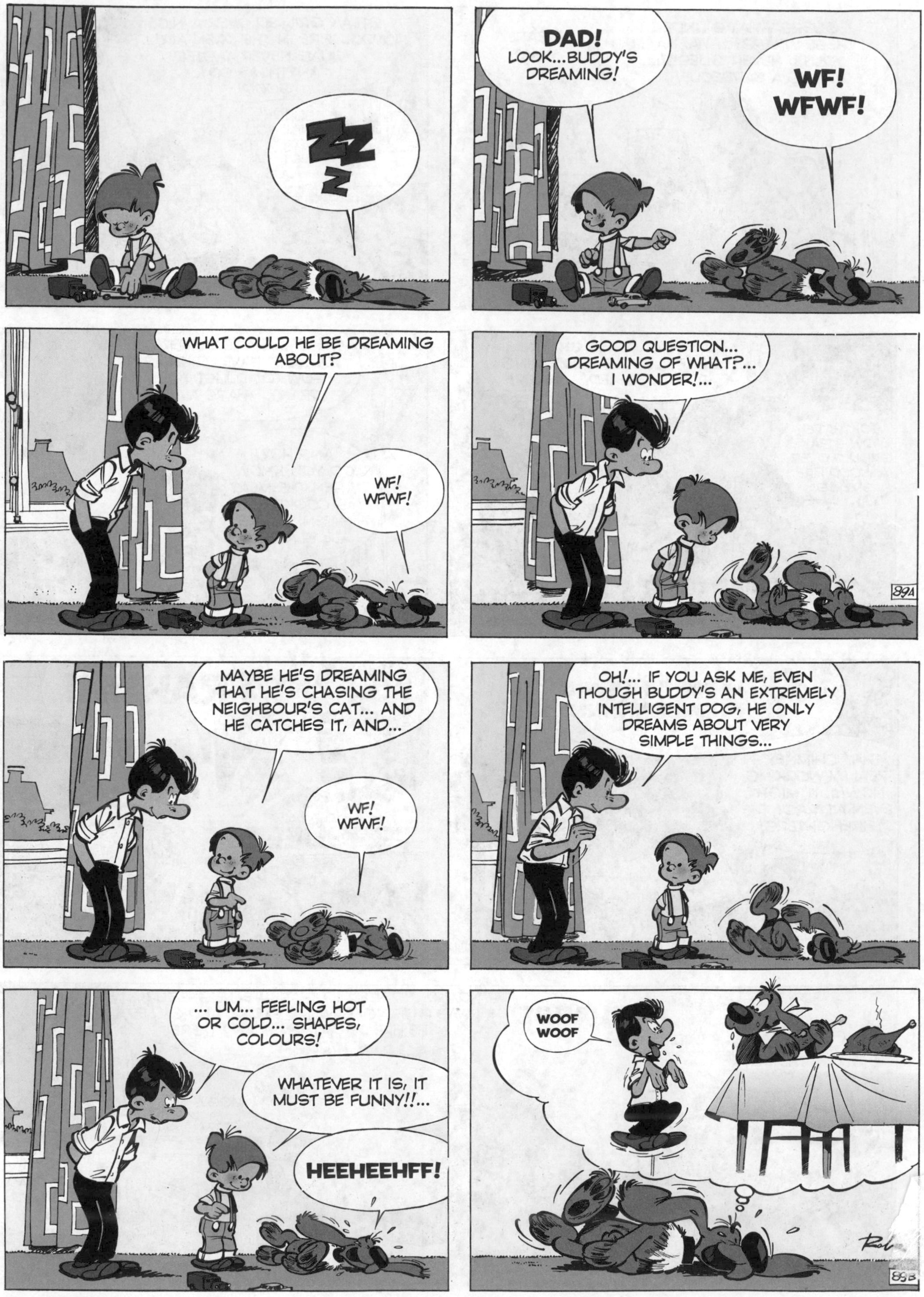

ZZZ
DAD! LOOK...BUDDY'S DREAMING!
WF! WFWF!
WHAT COULD HE BE DREAMING ABOUT?
WF! WFWF!
GOOD QUESTION... DREAMING OF WHAT?... I WONDER!...
MAYBE HE'S DREAMING THAT HE'S CHASING THE NEIGHBOUR'S CAT... AND HE CATCHES IT, AND...
WF! WFWF!
OH!... IF YOU ASK ME, EVEN THOUGH BUDDY'S AN EXTREMELY INTELLIGENT DOG, HE ONLY DREAMS ABOUT VERY SIMPLE THINGS...
... UM... FEELING HOT OR COLD... SHAPES, COLOURS!
WHATEVER IT IS, IT MUST BE FUNNY!!...
HEEHEEHFF!
WOOF WOOF

United for a Night

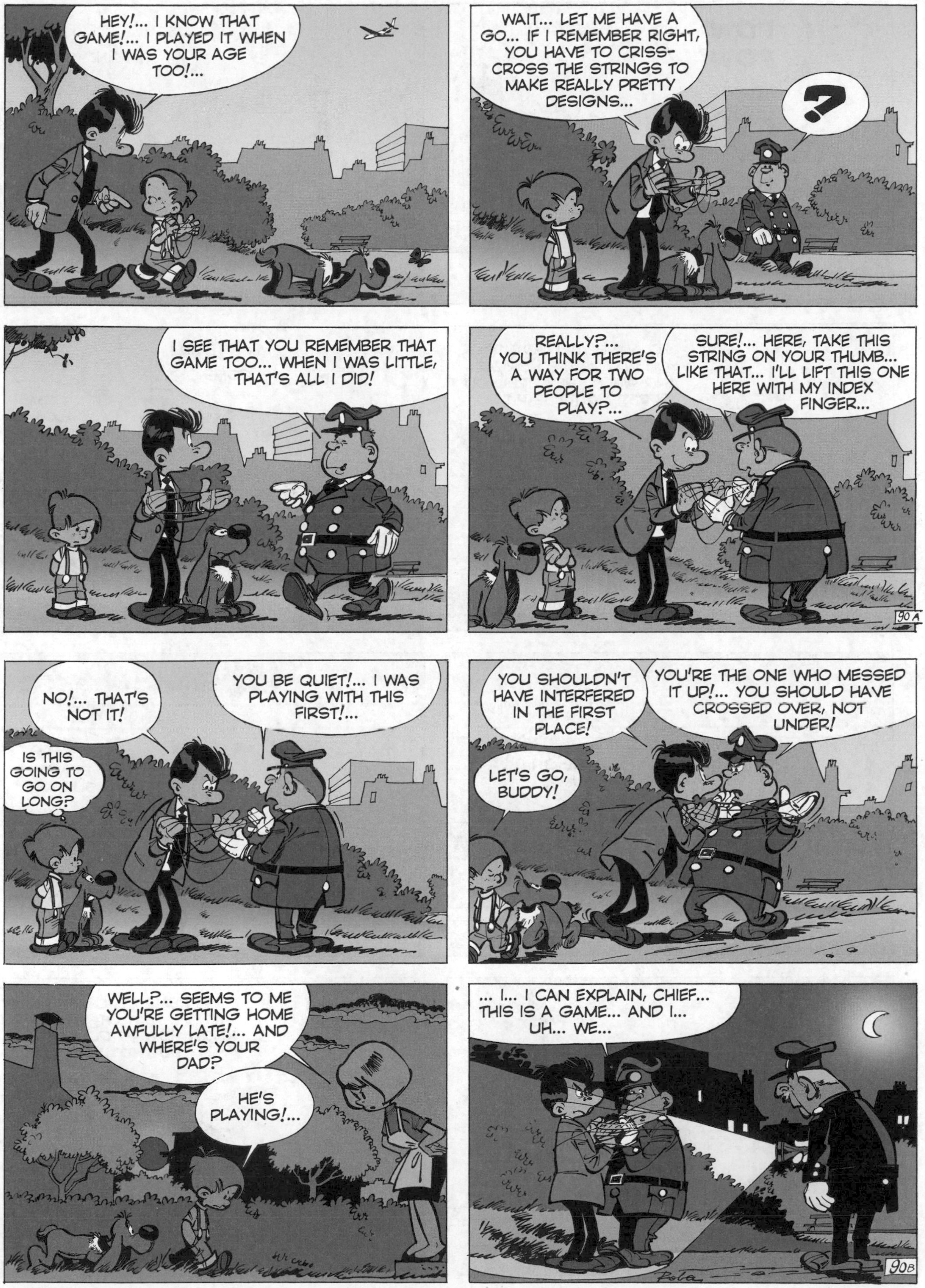

HEY!... I KNOW THAT GAME!... I PLAYED IT WHEN I WAS YOUR AGE TOO!...
WAIT... LET ME HAVE A GO... IF I REMEMBER RIGHT, YOU HAVE TO CRISS-CROSS THE STRINGS TO MAKE REALLY PRETTY DESIGNS...
?
I SEE THAT YOU REMEMBER THAT GAME TOO... WHEN I WAS LITTLE, THAT'S ALL I DID!
REALLY?... YOU THINK THERE'S A WAY FOR TWO PEOPLE TO PLAY?...
SURE!... HERE, TAKE THIS STRING ON YOUR THUMB... LIKE THAT... I'LL LIFT THIS ONE HERE WITH MY INDEX FINGER...
90 A
NO!... THAT'S NOT IT!
YOU BE QUIET!... I WAS PLAYING WITH THIS FIRST!...
IS THIS GOING TO GO ON LONG?
YOU SHOULDN'T HAVE INTERFERED IN THE FIRST PLACE!
YOU'RE THE ONE WHO MESSED IT UP!... YOU SHOULD HAVE CROSSED OVER, NOT UNDER!
LET'S GO, BUDDY!
WELL?... SEEMS TO ME YOU'RE GETTING HOME AWFULLY LATE!... AND WHERE'S YOUR DAD?
HE'S PLAYING!...
... I... I CAN EXPLAIN, CHIEF... THIS IS A GAME... AND I... UH... WE...
90B

Circus Dog

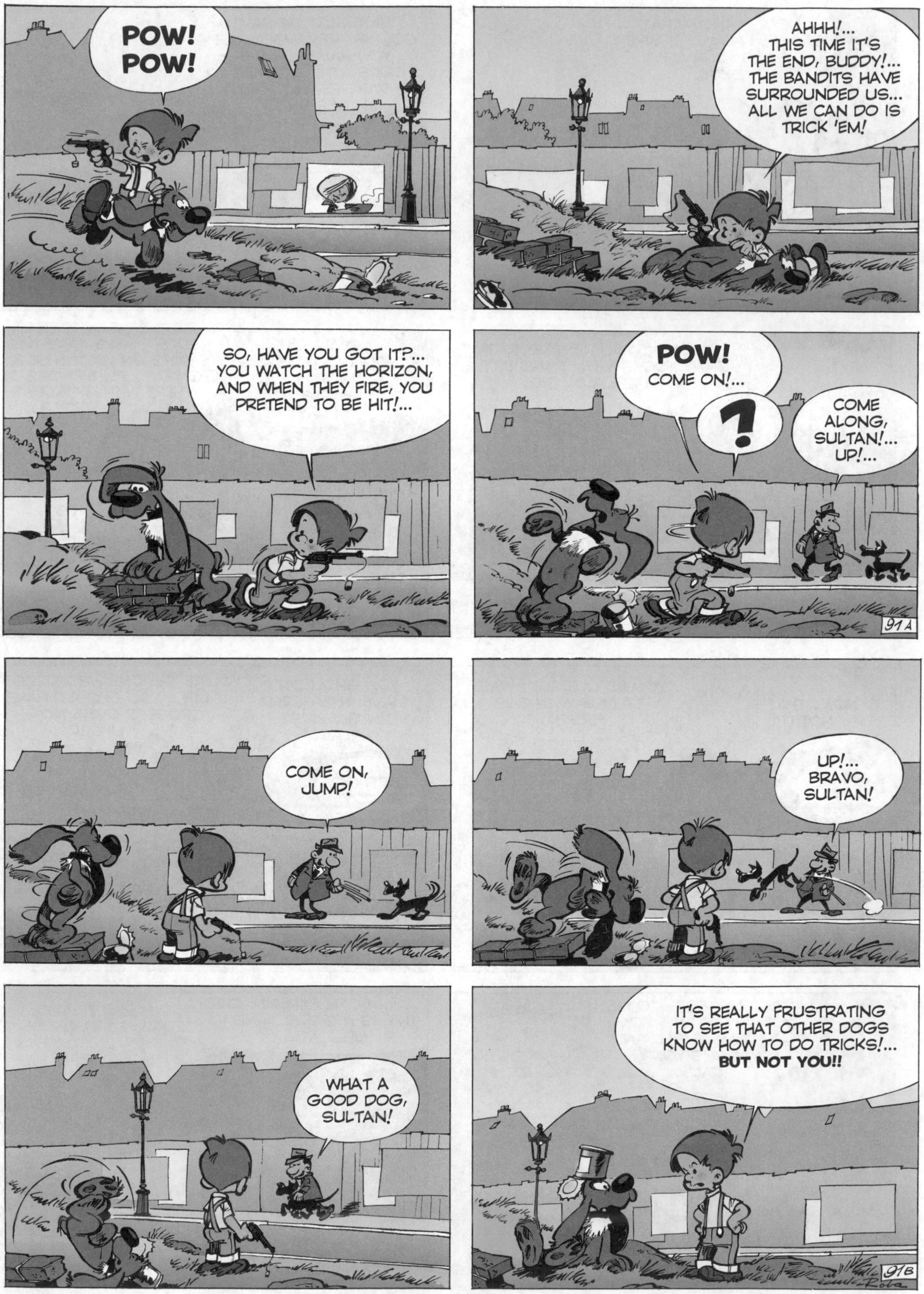
POW! POW!
AHHH!... THIS TIME IT'S THE END, BUDDY!... THE BANDITS HAVE SURROUNDED US... ALL WE CAN DO IS TRICK 'EM!
SO, HAVE YOU GOT IT?... YOU WATCH THE HORIZON, AND WHEN THEY FIRE, YOU PRETEND TO BE HIT!...
POW!
COME ON!...
?
COME ALONG, SULTAN!... UP!...
91 A
COME ON, JUMP!
UP!... BRAVO, SULTAN!
WHAT A GOOD DOG, SULTAN!
IT'S REALLY FRUSTRATING TO SEE THAT OTHER DOGS KNOW HOW TO DO TRICKS!... **BUT NOT YOU!!**
91 B

Dress for the Occasion

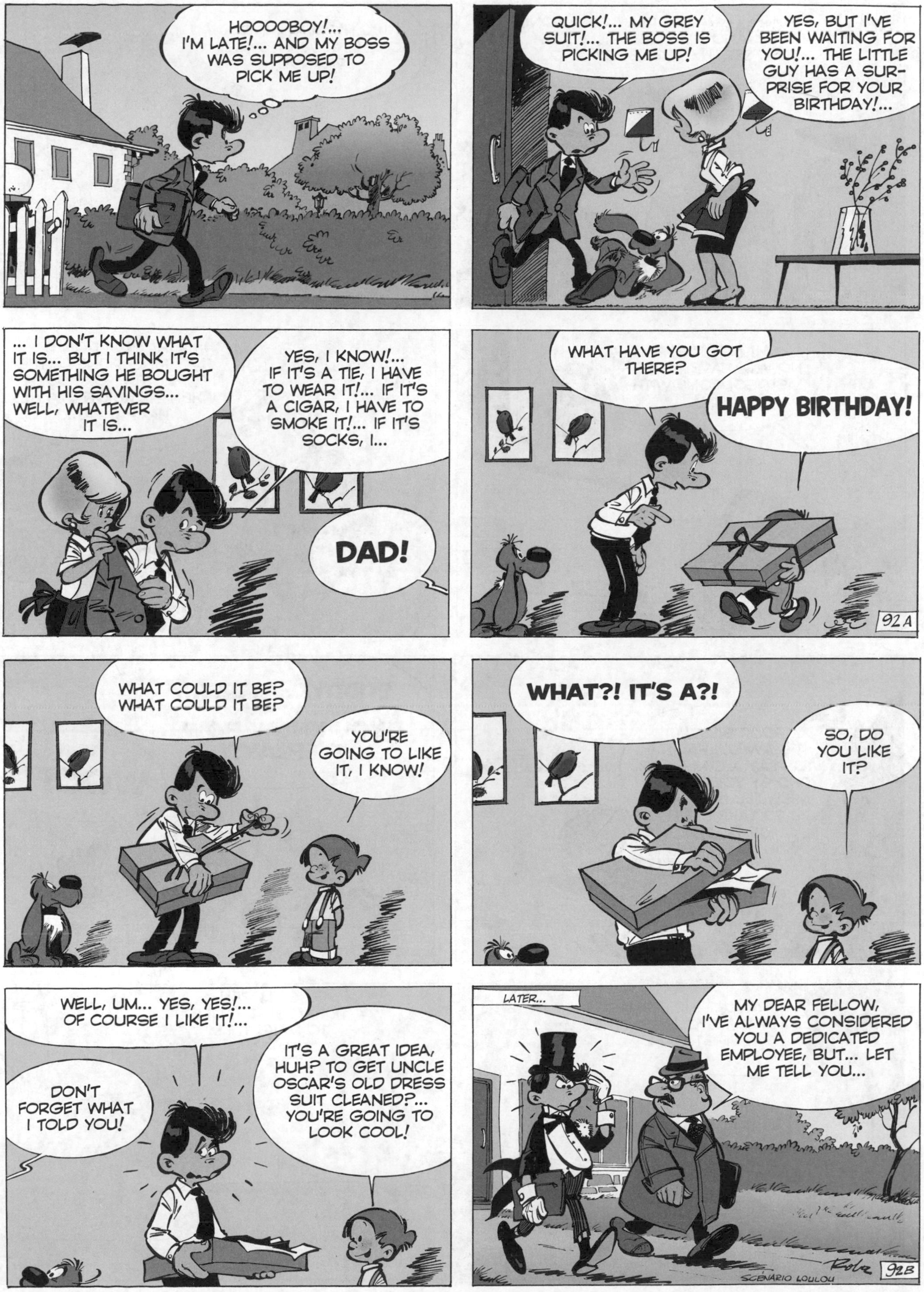

HOOOOBOY!... I'M LATE!... AND MY BOSS WAS SUPPOSED TO PICK ME UP!
QUICK!... MY GREY SUIT!... THE BOSS IS PICKING ME UP!
YES, BUT I'VE BEEN WAITING FOR YOU!... THE LITTLE GUY HAS A SURPRISE FOR YOUR BIRTHDAY!...
... I DON'T KNOW WHAT IT IS... BUT I THINK IT'S SOMETHING HE BOUGHT WITH HIS SAVINGS... WELL, WHATEVER IT IS...
YES, I KNOW!... IF IT'S A TIE, I HAVE TO WEAR IT!... IF IT'S A CIGAR, I HAVE TO SMOKE IT!... IF IT'S SOCKS, I...
DAD!
WHAT HAVE YOU GOT THERE?
HAPPY BIRTHDAY!
92A
WHAT COULD IT BE? WHAT COULD IT BE?
YOU'RE GOING TO LIKE IT, I KNOW!
WHAT?! IT'S A?!
SO, DO YOU LIKE IT?
WELL, UM... YES, YES!... OF COURSE I LIKE IT!...
DON'T FORGET WHAT I TOLD YOU!
IT'S A GREAT IDEA, HUH? TO GET UNCLE OSCAR'S OLD DRESS SUIT CLEANED?... YOU'RE GOING TO LOOK COOL!
LATER...
MY DEAR FELLOW, I'VE ALWAYS CONSIDERED YOU A DEDICATED EMPLOYEE, BUT... LET ME TELL YOU...
Roba 92B
SCENARIO LOULOU

The Partner

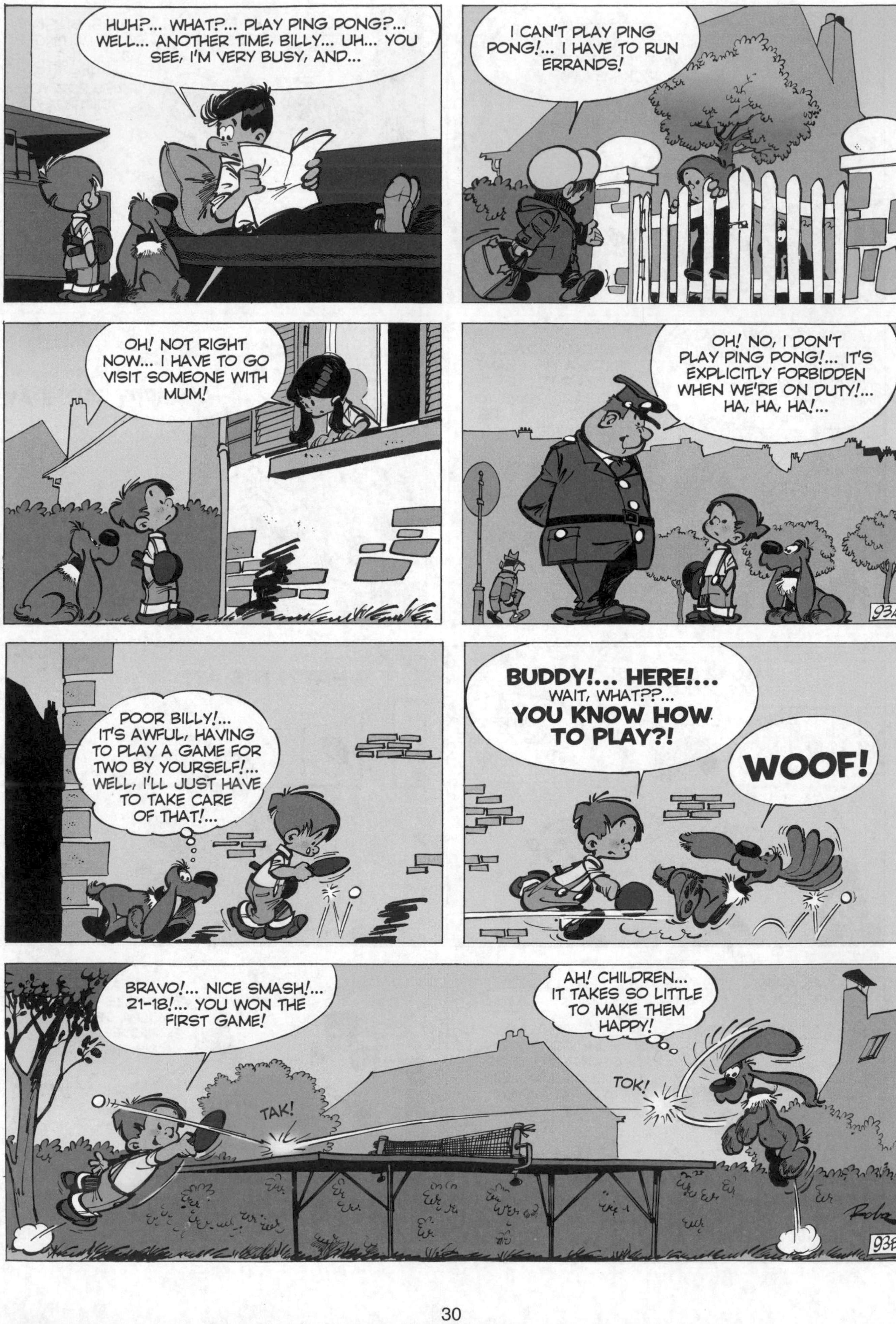

HUH?... WHAT?... PLAY PING PONG?... WELL... ANOTHER TIME, BILLY... UH... YOU SEE, I'M VERY BUSY, AND...
I CAN'T PLAY PING PONG!... I HAVE TO RUN ERRANDS!
OH! NOT RIGHT NOW... I HAVE TO GO VISIT SOMEONE WITH MUM!
OH! NO, I DON'T PLAY PING PONG!... IT'S EXPLICITLY FORBIDDEN WHEN WE'RE ON DUTY!... HA, HA, HA!...
93A
POOR BILLY!... IT'S AWFUL, HAVING TO PLAY A GAME FOR TWO BY YOURSELF!... WELL, I'LL JUST HAVE TO TAKE CARE OF THAT!...
BUDDY!... HERE!... WAIT, WHAT??... YOU KNOW HOW TO PLAY?!
WOOF!
BRAVO!... NICE SMASH!... 21-18!... YOU WON THE FIRST GAME!
AH! CHILDREN... IT TAKES SO LITTLE TO MAKE THEM HAPPY!
TAK!
TOK!
Roba
93B

The Stylist

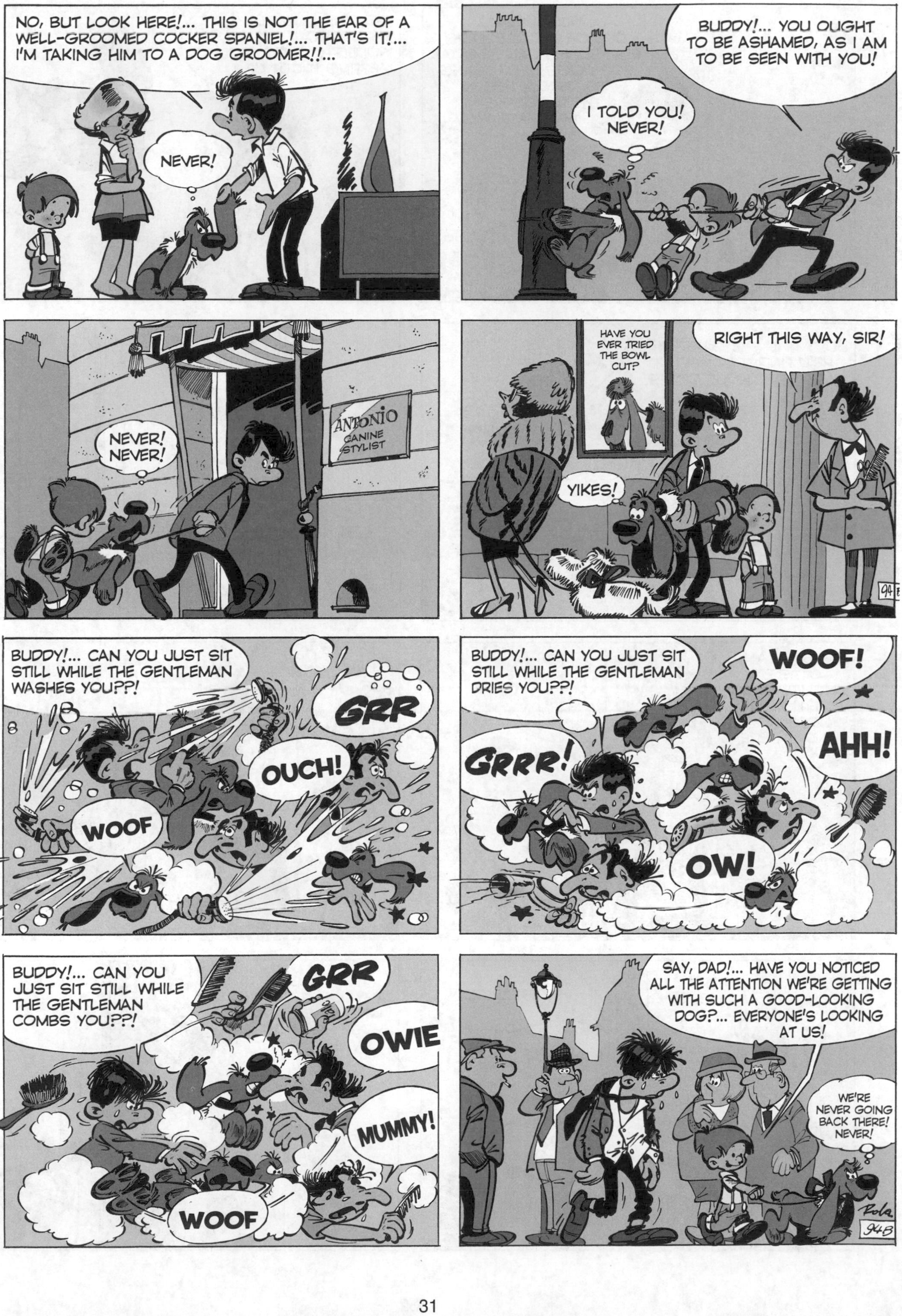
NO, BUT LOOK HERE!... THIS IS NOT THE EAR OF A WELL-GROOMED COCKER SPANIEL!... THAT'S IT!... I'M TAKING HIM TO A DOG GROOMER!!...
NEVER!
BUDDY!... YOU OUGHT TO BE ASHAMED, AS I AM TO BE SEEN WITH YOU!
I TOLD YOU! NEVER!
ANTONIO CANINE STYLIST
NEVER! NEVER!
HAVE YOU EVER TRIED THE BOWL CUT?
RIGHT THIS WAY, SIR!
YIKES!
BUDDY!... CAN YOU JUST SIT STILL WHILE THE GENTLEMAN WASHES YOU??!
GRR
OUCH!
WOOF
BUDDY!... CAN YOU JUST SIT STILL WHILE THE GENTLEMAN DRIES YOU??!
WOOF!
GRRR!
AHH!
OW!
BUDDY!... CAN YOU JUST SIT STILL WHILE THE GENTLEMAN COMBS YOU??!
GRR
OWIE
MUMMY!
WOOF
SAY, DAD!... HAVE YOU NOTICED ALL THE ATTENTION WE'RE GETTING WITH SUCH A GOOD-LOOKING DOG?... EVERYONE'S LOOKING AT US!
WE'RE NEVER GOING BACK THERE! NEVER!

Getting a Backbone

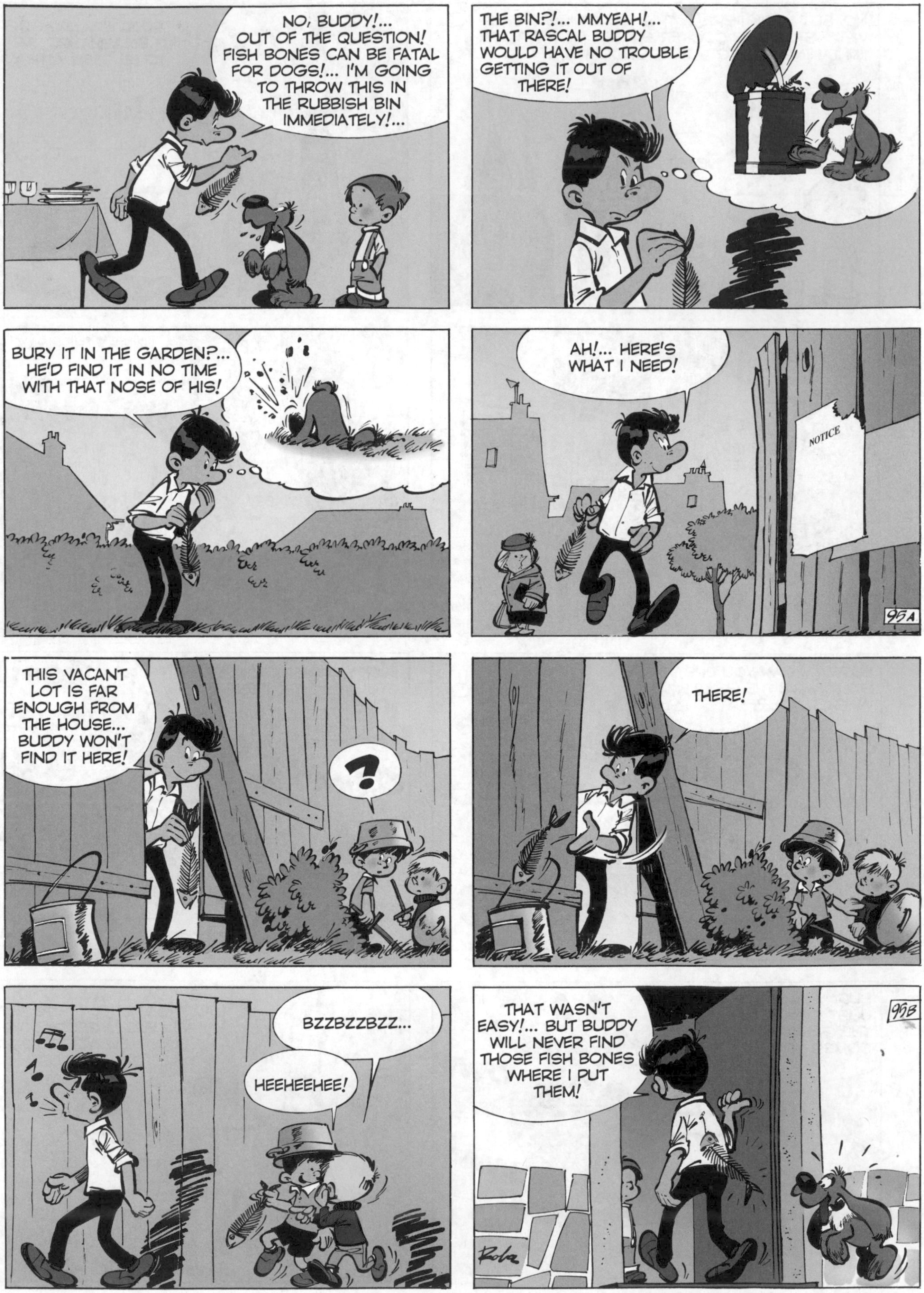

NO, BUDDY!... OUT OF THE QUESTION! FISH BONES CAN BE FATAL FOR DOGS!... I'M GOING TO THROW THIS IN THE RUBBISH BIN IMMEDIATELY!...
THE BIN?!... MMYEAH!... THAT RASCAL BUDDY WOULD HAVE NO TROUBLE GETTING IT OUT OF THERE!
BURY IT IN THE GARDEN?... HE'D FIND IT IN NO TIME WITH THAT NOSE OF HIS!
AH!... HERE'S WHAT I NEED!
NOTICE
95A
THIS VACANT LOT IS FAR ENOUGH FROM THE HOUSE... BUDDY WON'T FIND IT HERE!
?
THERE!
BZZBZZBZZ...
HEEHEEHEE!
THAT WASN'T EASY!... BUT BUDDY WILL NEVER FIND THOSE FISH BONES WHERE I PUT THEM!
95B
Roba

Toothache

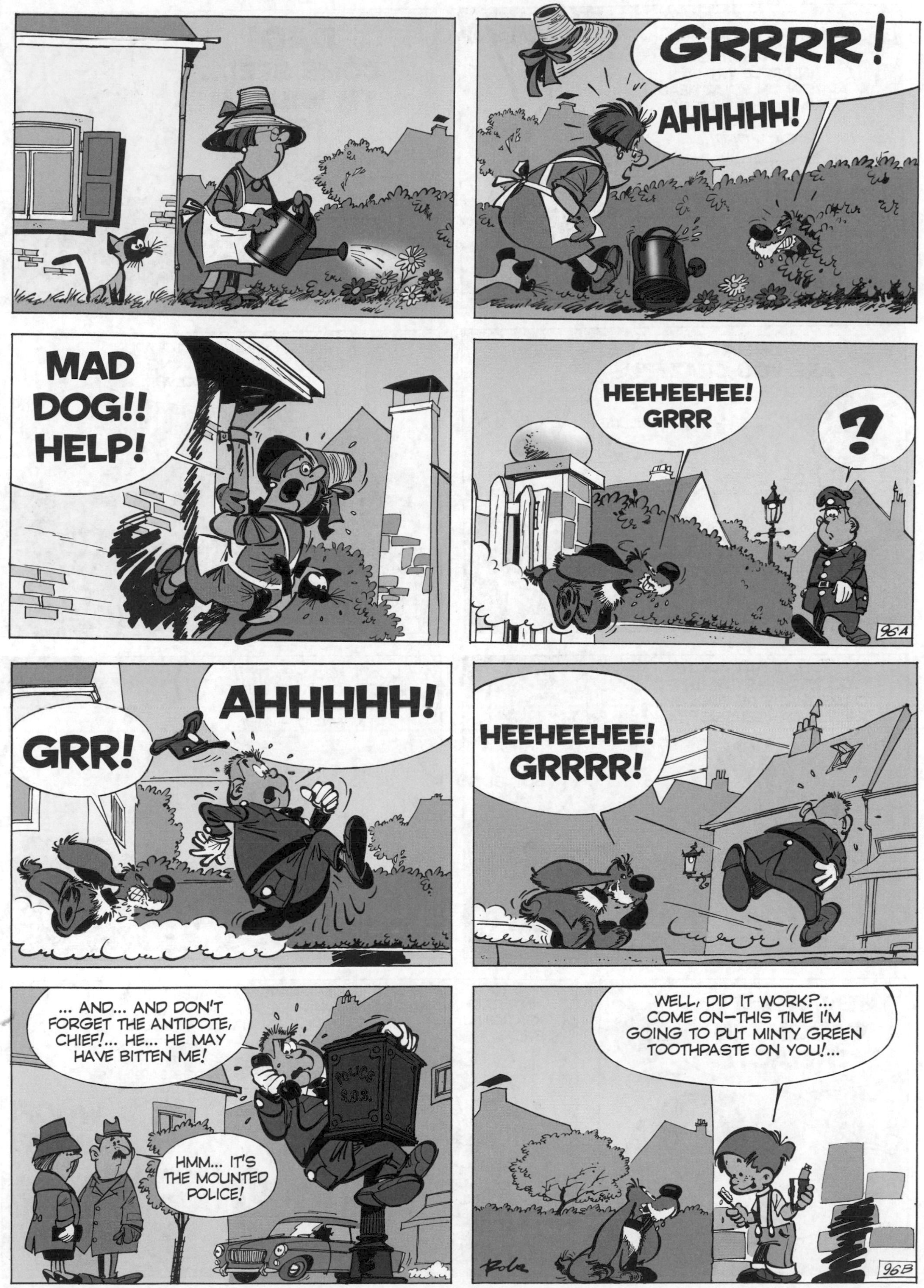
GRRRR!
AHHHHH!
MAD DOG!! HELP!
HEEHEEHEE! GRRR
?
96A
AHHHHH!
GRR!
HEEHEEHEE! GRRRR!
... AND... AND DON'T FORGET THE ANTIDOTE, CHIEF!... HE... HE MAY HAVE BITTEN ME!
POLICE S.O.S.
HMM... IT'S THE MOUNTED POLICE!
WELL, DID IT WORK?... COME ON—THIS TIME I'M GOING TO PUT MINTY GREEN TOOTHPASTE ON YOU!...
Roba
96B

The Apple of His Eye

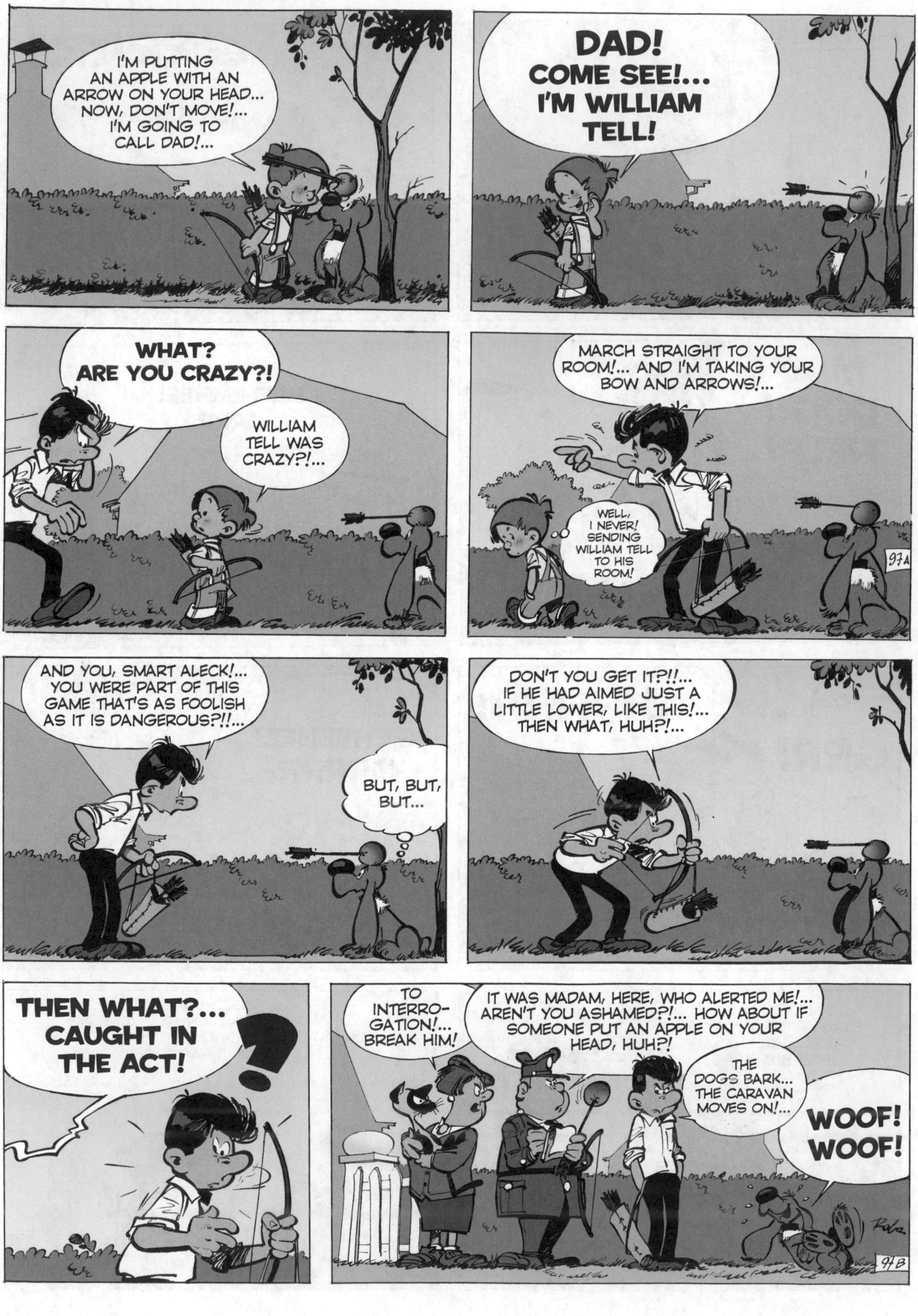
I'M PUTTING AN APPLE WITH AN ARROW ON YOUR HEAD... NOW, DON'T MOVE!... I'M GOING TO CALL DAD!...
DAD! COME SEE!... I'M WILLIAM TELL!
WHAT? ARE YOU CRAZY?!
WILLIAM TELL WAS CRAZY?!...
MARCH STRAIGHT TO YOUR ROOM!... AND I'M TAKING YOUR BOW AND ARROWS!...
WELL, I NEVER! SENDING WILLIAM TELL TO HIS ROOM!
97A
AND YOU, SMART ALECK!... YOU WERE PART OF THIS GAME THAT'S AS FOOLISH AS IT IS DANGEROUS?!!...
BUT, BUT, BUT...
DON'T YOU GET IT?!!... IF HE HAD AIMED JUST A LITTLE LOWER, LIKE THIS!... THEN WHAT, HUH?!...
THEN WHAT?... CAUGHT IN THE ACT!
TO INTERROGATION!... BREAK HIM!
IT WAS MADAM, HERE, WHO ALERTED ME!... AREN'T YOU ASHAMED?!... HOW ABOUT IF SOMEONE PUT AN APPLE ON YOUR HEAD, HUH?!
THE DOGS BARK... THE CARAVAN MOVES ON!...
WOOF! WOOF!
Roba
97B

Liability Coverage

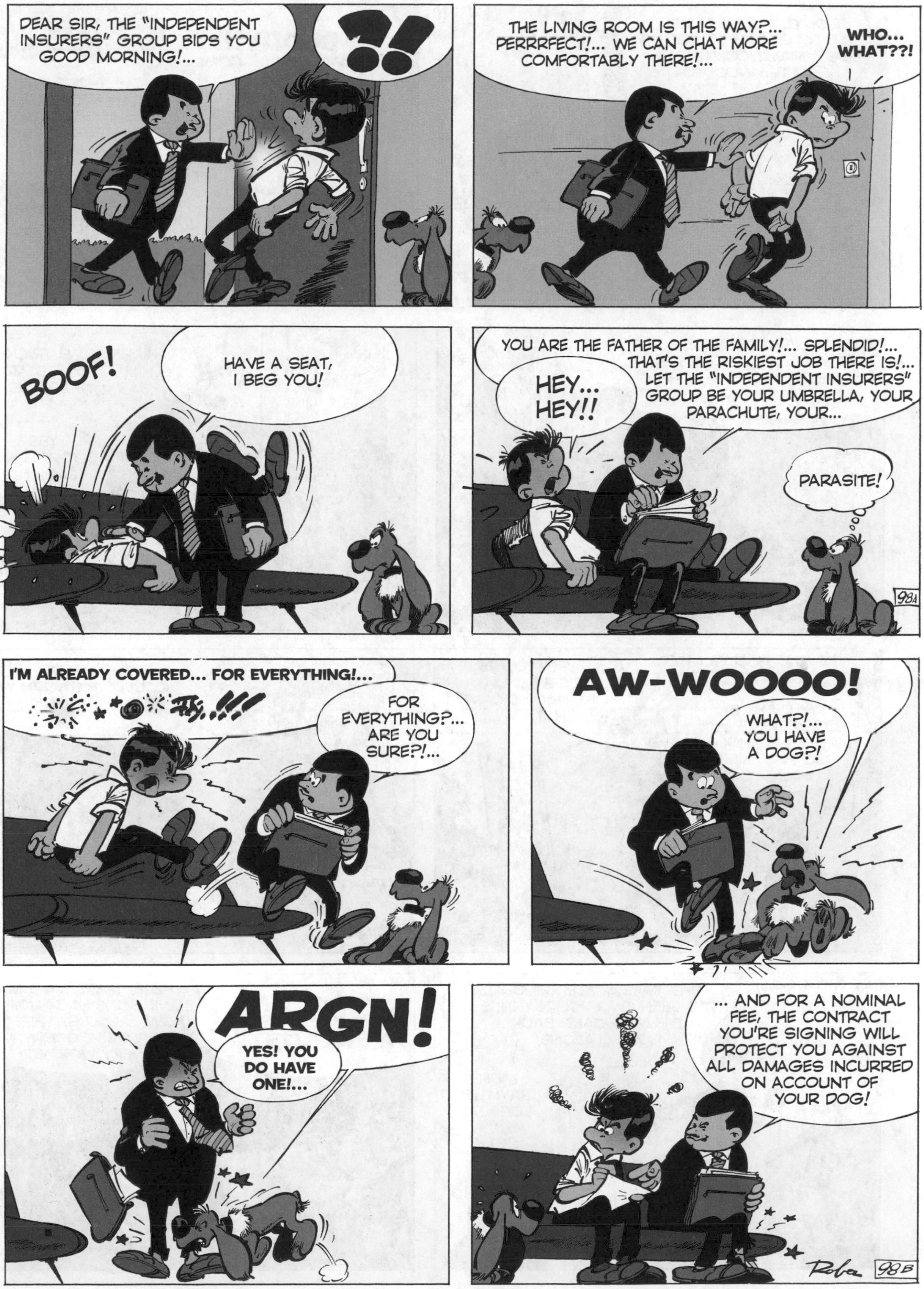
DEAR SIR, THE "INDEPENDENT INSURERS" GROUP BIDS YOU GOOD MORNING!...
THE LIVING ROOM IS THIS WAY?... PERRRFECT!... WE CAN CHAT MORE COMFORTABLY THERE!...
WHO... WHAT??!
BOOF!
HAVE A SEAT, I BEG YOU!
YOU ARE THE FATHER OF THE FAMILY!... SPLENDID!... THAT'S THE RISKIEST JOB THERE IS!... LET THE "INDEPENDENT INSURERS" GROUP BE YOUR UMBRELLA, YOUR PARACHUTE, YOUR...
HEY... HEY!!
PARASITE!
98A
I'M ALREADY COVERED... FOR EVERYTHING!...
FOR EVERYTHING?... ARE YOU SURE?!...
AW-WOOOO!
WHAT?!... YOU HAVE A DOG?!
ARGN!
YES! YOU DO HAVE ONE!...
... AND FOR A NOMINAL FEE, THE CONTRACT YOU'RE SIGNING WILL PROTECT YOU AGAINST ALL DAMAGES INCURRED ON ACCOUNT OF YOUR DOG!
Roba
98B

Deep in the Woods

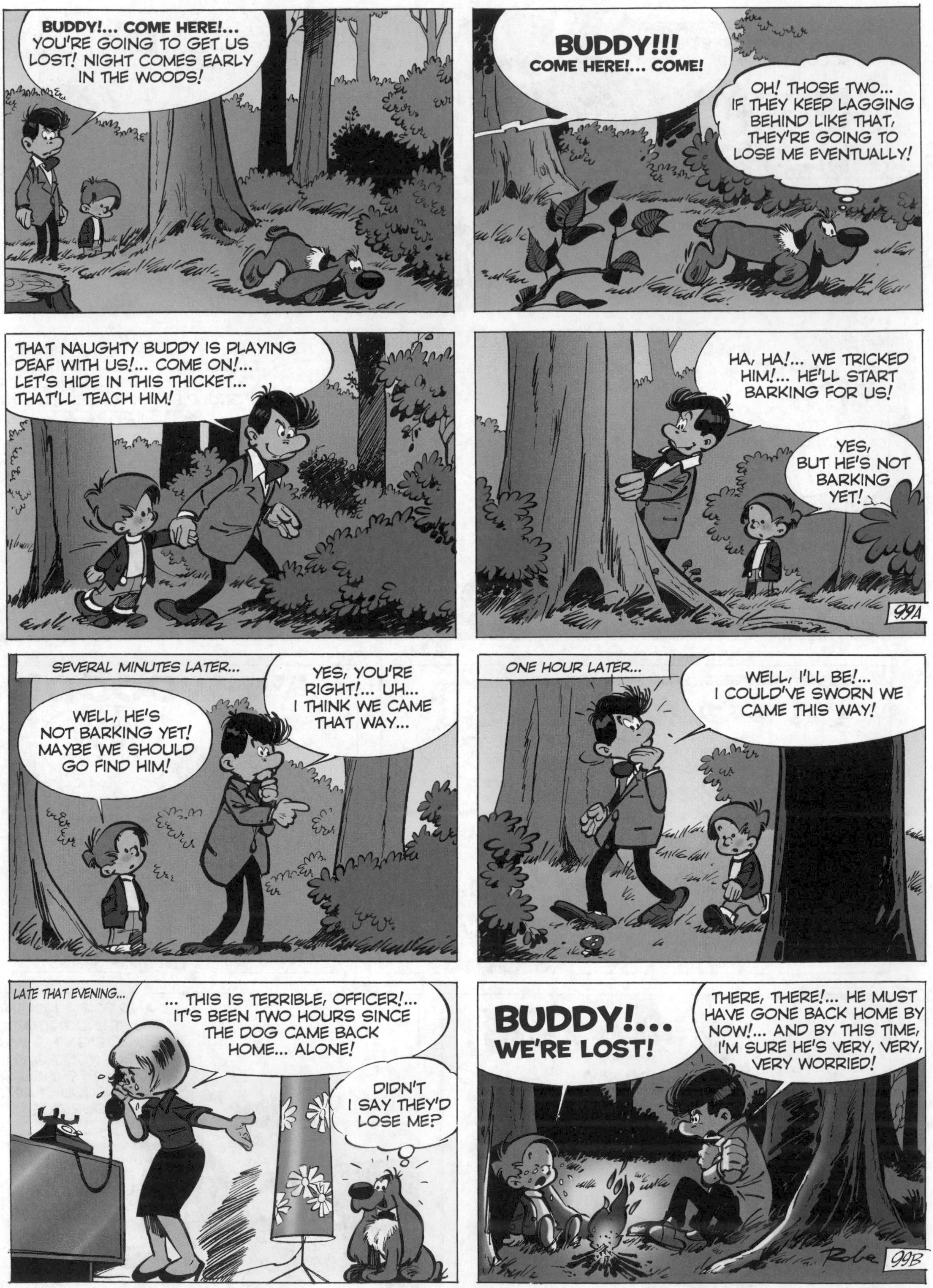

BUDDY!... COME HERE!... YOU'RE GOING TO GET US LOST! NIGHT COMES EARLY IN THE WOODS!
BUDDY!!! COME HERE!... COME!
OH! THOSE TWO... IF THEY KEEP LAGGING BEHIND LIKE THAT, THEY'RE GOING TO LOSE ME EVENTUALLY!
THAT NAUGHTY BUDDY IS PLAYING DEAF WITH US!... COME ON!... LET'S HIDE IN THIS THICKET... THAT'LL TEACH HIM!
HA, HA!... WE TRICKED HIM!... HE'LL START BARKING FOR US!
YES, BUT HE'S NOT BARKING YET!
99A
SEVERAL MINUTES LATER...
WELL, HE'S NOT BARKING YET! MAYBE WE SHOULD GO FIND HIM!
YES, YOU'RE RIGHT!... UH... I THINK WE CAME THAT WAY...
ONE HOUR LATER...
WELL, I'LL BE!... I COULD'VE SWORN WE CAME THIS WAY!
LATE THAT EVENING...
... THIS IS TERRIBLE, OFFICER!... IT'S BEEN TWO HOURS SINCE THE DOG CAME BACK HOME... ALONE!
DIDN'T I SAY THEY'D LOSE ME?
BUDDY!... WE'RE LOST!
THERE, THERE!... HE MUST HAVE GONE BACK HOME BY NOW!... AND BY THIS TIME, I'M SURE HE'S VERY, VERY, VERY WORRIED!
Roba
99B

Dad Gets Treed!

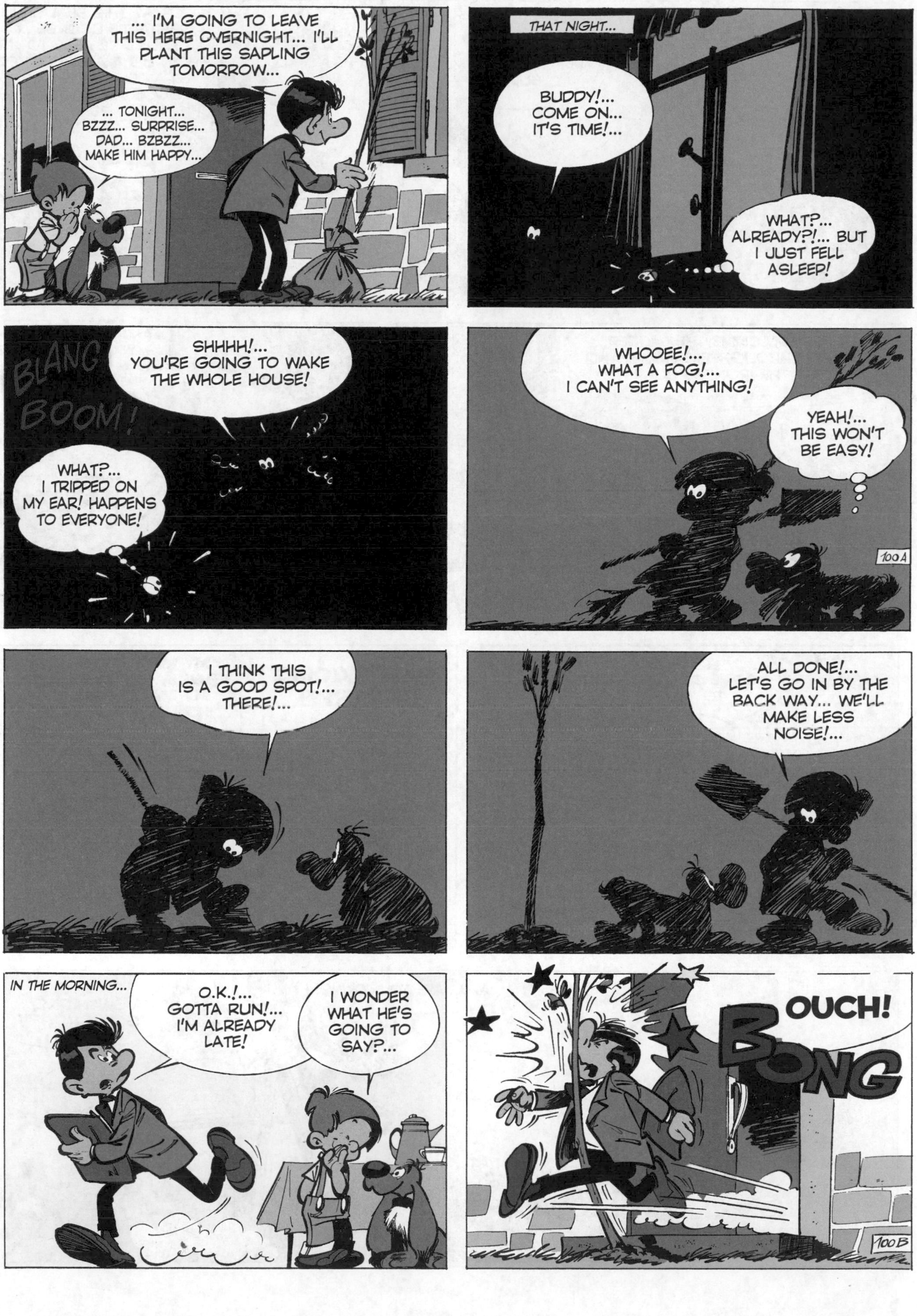

... I'M GOING TO LEAVE THIS HERE OVERNIGHT... I'LL PLANT THIS SAPLING TOMORROW...
... TONIGHT... BZZZ... SURPRISE... DAD... BZBZZ... MAKE HIM HAPPY...
THAT NIGHT...
BUDDY!... COME ON... IT'S TIME!...
WHAT?... ALREADY?!... BUT I JUST FELL ASLEEP!
BLANG
BOOM!
SHHHH!... YOU'RE GOING TO WAKE THE WHOLE HOUSE!
WHAT?... I TRIPPED ON MY EAR! HAPPENS TO EVERYONE!
WHOOEE!... WHAT A FOG!... I CAN'T SEE ANYTHING!
YEAH!... THIS WON'T BE EASY!
100 A
I THINK THIS IS A GOOD SPOT!... THERE!...
ALL DONE!... LET'S GO IN BY THE BACK WAY... WE'LL MAKE LESS NOISE!...
IN THE MORNING...
O.K.!... GOTTA RUN!... I'M ALREADY LATE!
I WONDER WHAT HE'S GOING TO SAY?...
OUCH!
BONG
100 B

Obstacle Course

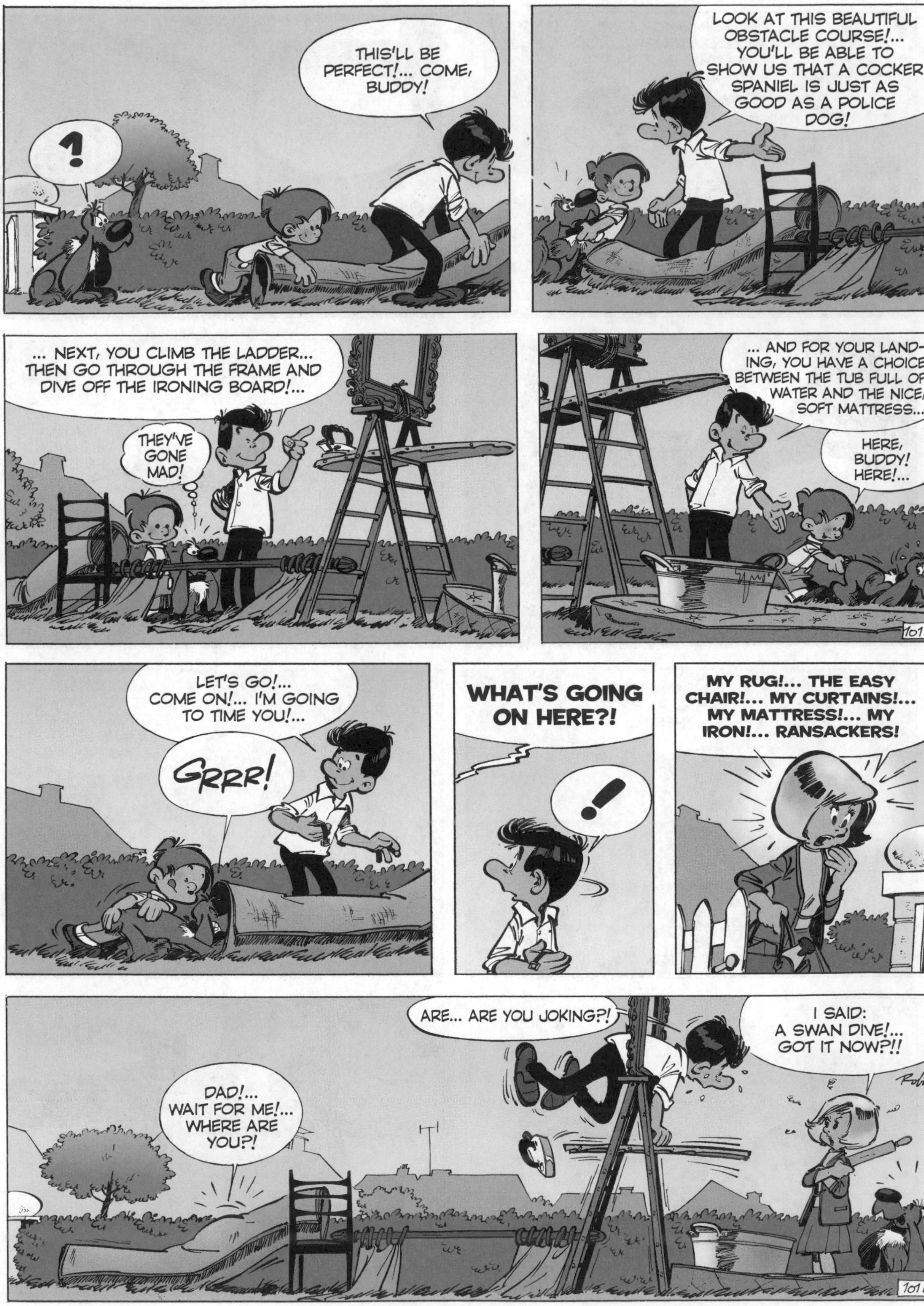

?
THIS'LL BE PERFECT!... COME, BUDDY!
LOOK AT THIS BEAUTIFUL OBSTACLE COURSE!... YOU'LL BE ABLE TO SHOW US THAT A COCKER SPANIEL IS JUST AS GOOD AS A POLICE DOG!
... NEXT, YOU CLIMB THE LADDER... THEN GO THROUGH THE FRAME AND DIVE OFF THE IRONING BOARD!...
THEY'VE GONE MAD!
... AND FOR YOUR LANDING, YOU HAVE A CHOICE BETWEEN THE TUB FULL OF WATER AND THE NICE, SOFT MATTRESS...
HERE, BUDDY! HERE!...
101 A
LET'S GO!... COME ON!... I'M GOING TO TIME YOU!...
GRRR!
WHAT'S GOING ON HERE?!
!
MY RUG!... THE EASY CHAIR!... MY CURTAINS!... MY MATTRESS!... MY IRON!... RANSACKERS!
ARE... ARE YOU JOKING?!
I SAID: A SWAN DIVE!... GOT IT NOW?!!
DAD!... WAIT FOR ME!... WHERE ARE YOU?!
101 B

Delighted to See You

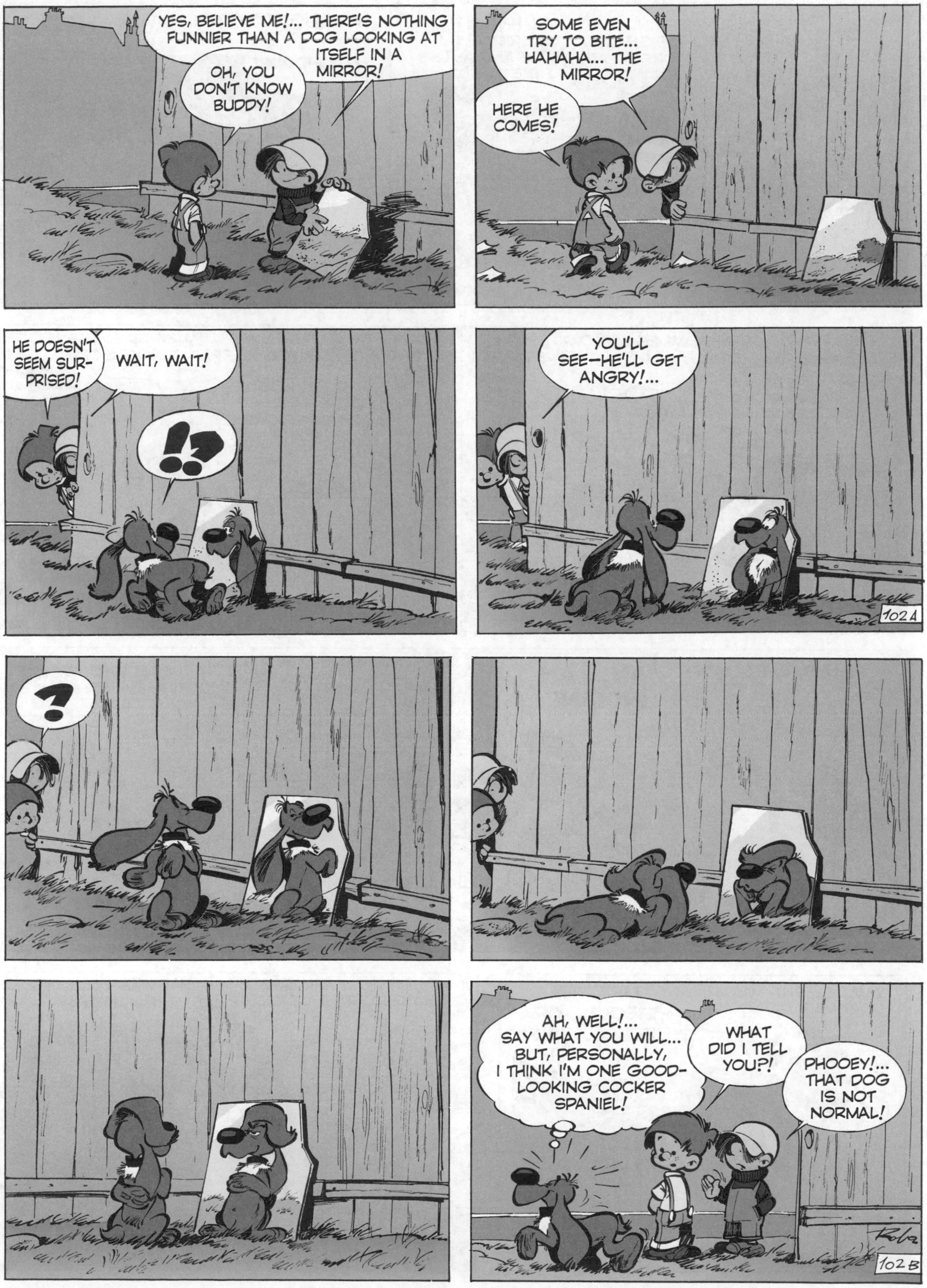
YES, BELIEVE ME!... THERE'S NOTHING FUNNIER THAN A DOG LOOKING AT ITSELF IN A MIRROR!
OH, YOU DON'T KNOW BUDDY!
SOME EVEN TRY TO BITE... HAHAHA... THE MIRROR!
HERE HE COMES!
HE DOESN'T SEEM SUR- PRISED!
WAIT, WAIT!
YOU'LL SEE—HE'LL GET ANGRY!...
102 A
AH, WELL!... SAY WHAT YOU WILL... BUT, PERSONALLY, I THINK I'M ONE GOOD- LOOKING COCKER SPANIEL!
WHAT DID I TELL YOU?!
PHOOEY!... THAT DOG IS NOT NORMAL!
Roba
102 B

The Squaw and the Sachem

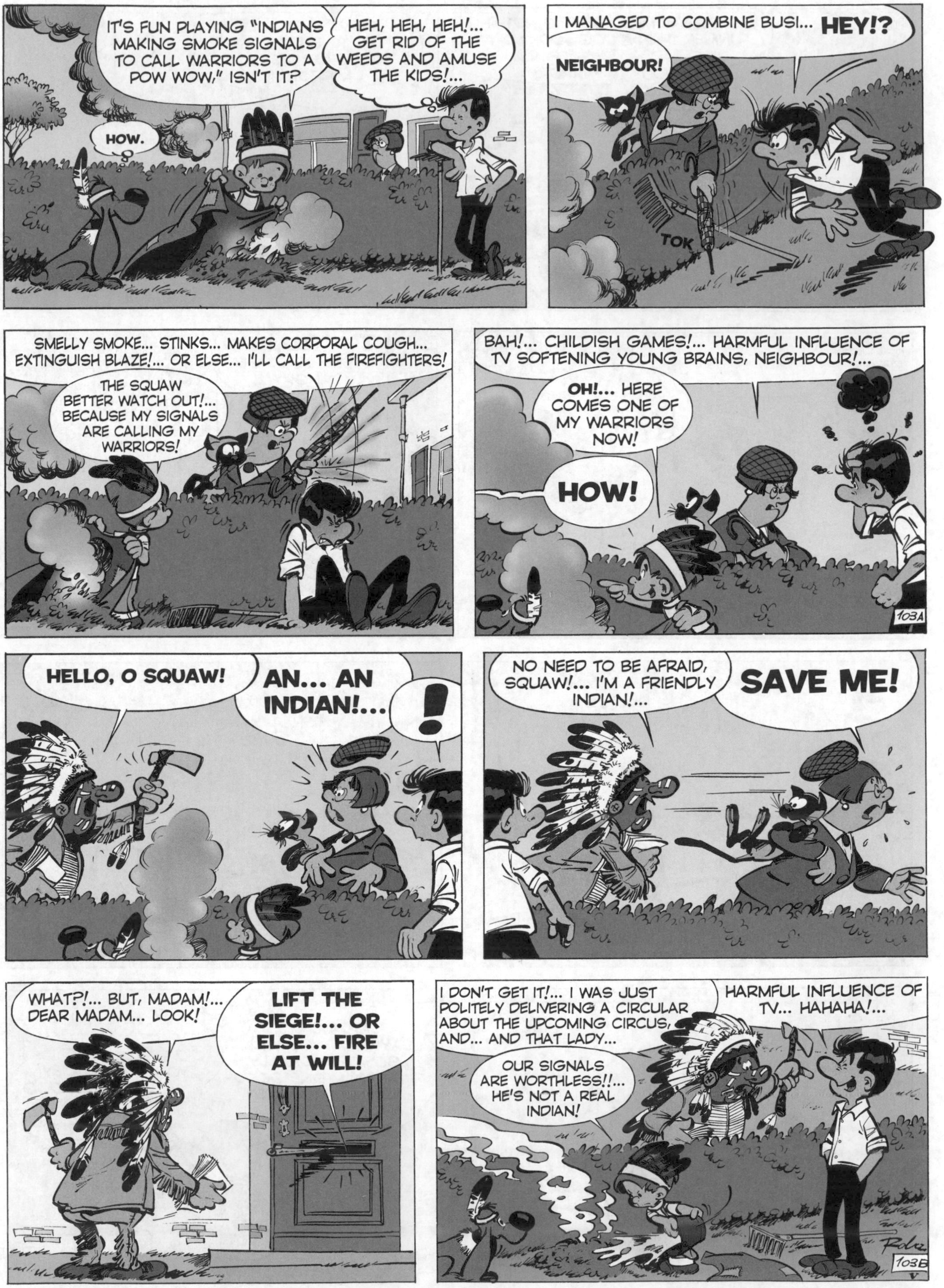

IT'S FUN PLAYING "INDIANS MAKING SMOKE SIGNALS TO CALL WARRIORS TO A POW WOW," ISN'T IT?
HEH, HEH, HEH!... GET RID OF THE WEEDS AND AMUSE THE KIDS!...
HOW.
I MANAGED TO COMBINE BUSI... HEY!?
NEIGHBOUR!
TOK
SMELLY SMOKE... STINKS... MAKES CORPORAL COUGH... EXTINGUISH BLAZE!... OR ELSE... I'LL CALL THE FIREFIGHTERS!
THE SQUAW BETTER WATCH OUT!... BECAUSE MY SIGNALS ARE CALLING MY WARRIORS!
BAH!... CHILDISH GAMES!... HARMFUL INFLUENCE OF TV SOFTENING YOUNG BRAINS, NEIGHBOUR!...
OH!... HERE COMES ONE OF MY WARRIORS NOW!
HOW!
103A
HELLO, O SQUAW!
AN... AN INDIAN!...
!
NO NEED TO BE AFRAID, SQUAW!... I'M A FRIENDLY INDIAN!...
SAVE ME!
WHAT?!... BUT, MADAM!... DEAR MADAM... LOOK!
LIFT THE SIEGE!... OR ELSE... FIRE AT WILL!
I DON'T GET IT!... I WAS JUST POLITELY DELIVERING A CIRCULAR ABOUT THE UPCOMING CIRCUS, AND... AND THAT LADY...
HARMFUL INFLUENCE OF TV... HAHAHA!...
OUR SIGNALS ARE WORTHLESS!!... HE'S NOT A REAL INDIAN!
Roba
103B

A Hunting Dog

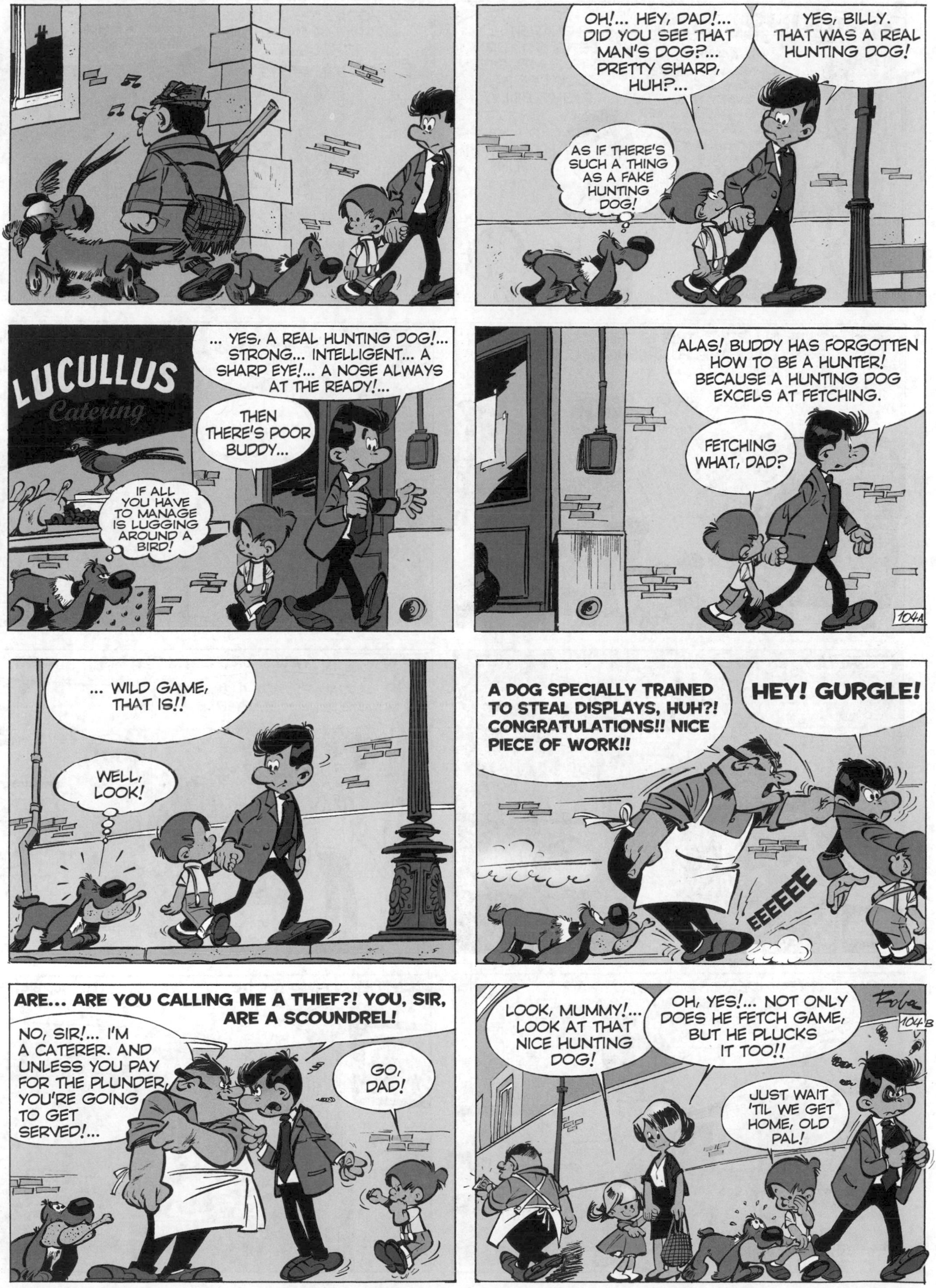
OH!... HEY, DAD!... DID YOU SEE THAT MAN'S DOG?... PRETTY SHARP, HUH?...
YES, BILLY. THAT WAS A REAL HUNTING DOG!
AS IF THERE'S SUCH A THING AS A FAKE HUNTING DOG!
LUCULLUS
Catering
... YES, A REAL HUNTING DOG!... STRONG... INTELLIGENT... A SHARP EYE!... A NOSE ALWAYS AT THE READY!...
THEN THERE'S POOR BUDDY...
IF ALL YOU HAVE TO MANAGE IS LUGGING AROUND A BIRD!
ALAS! BUDDY HAS FORGOTTEN HOW TO BE A HUNTER! BECAUSE A HUNTING DOG EXCELS AT FETCHING.
FETCHING WHAT, DAD?
104A
... WILD GAME, THAT IS!!
WELL, LOOK!
A DOG SPECIALLY TRAINED TO STEAL DISPLAYS, HUH?! CONGRATULATIONS!! NICE PIECE OF WORK!!
HEY! GURGLE!
EEEEEE
ARE... ARE YOU CALLING ME A THIEF?! YOU, SIR, ARE A SCOUNDREL!
NO, SIR!... I'M A CATERER. AND UNLESS YOU PAY FOR THE PLUNDER, YOU'RE GOING TO GET SERVED!...
GO, DAD!
LOOK, MUMMY!... LOOK AT THAT NICE HUNTING DOG!
OH, YES!... NOT ONLY DOES HE FETCH GAME, BUT HE PLUCKS IT TOO!!
JUST WAIT 'TIL WE GET HOME, OLD PAL!
Roba
104B

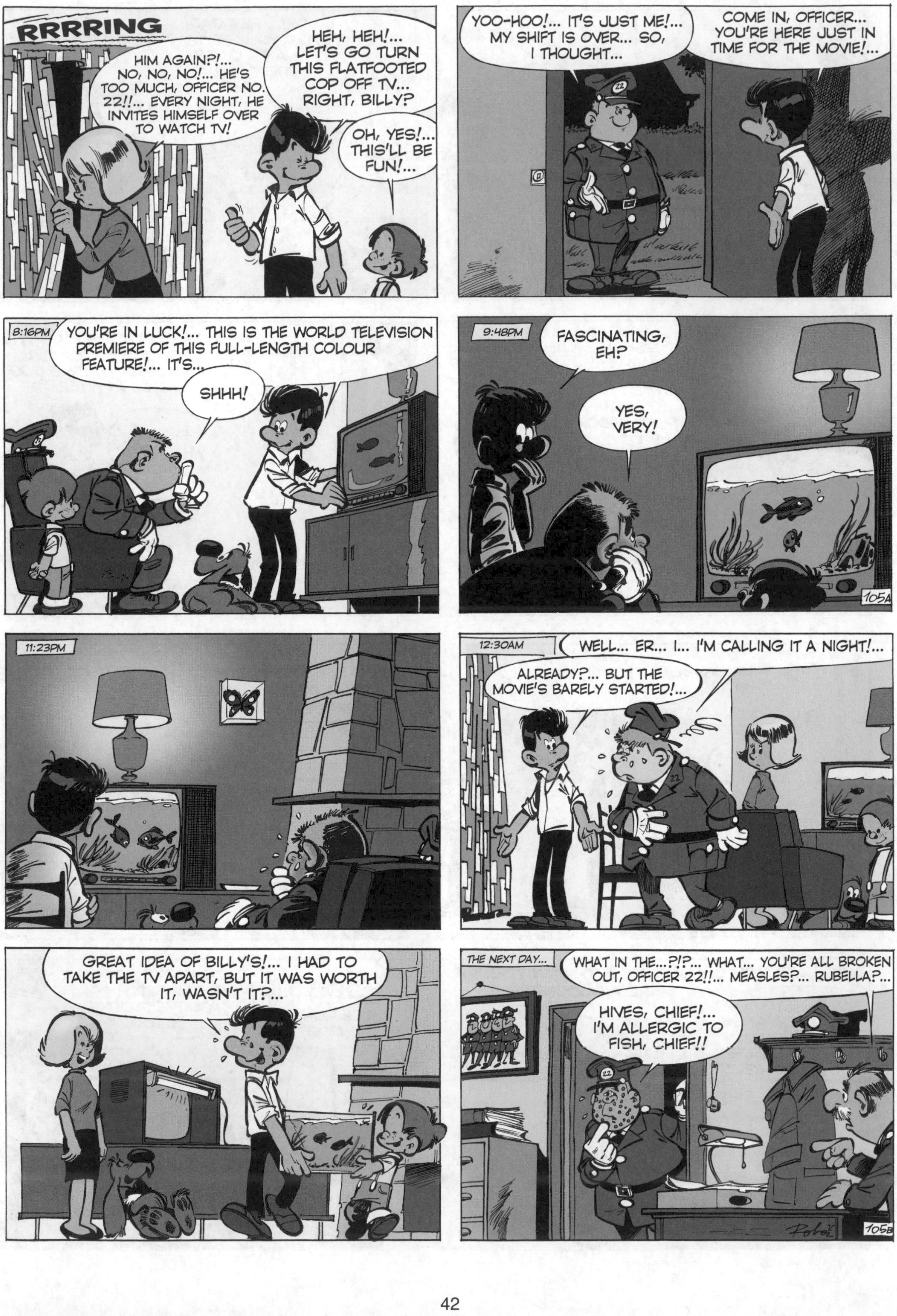
RRRRING
HIM AGAIN?!... NO, NO, NO!... HE'S TOO MUCH, OFFICER NO. 22!!... EVERY NIGHT, HE INVITES HIMSELF OVER TO WATCH TV!
HEH, HEH!... LET'S GO TURN THIS FLATFOOTED COP OFF TV... RIGHT, BILLY?
OH, YES!... THIS'LL BE FUN!...
YOO-HOO!... IT'S JUST ME!... MY SHIFT IS OVER... SO, I THOUGHT...
COME IN, OFFICER... YOU'RE HERE JUST IN TIME FOR THE MOVIE!...
8:16PM
YOU'RE IN LUCK!... THIS IS THE WORLD TELEVISION PREMIERE OF THIS FULL-LENGTH COLOUR FEATURE!... IT'S...
SHHH!
9:48PM
FASCINATING, EH?
YES, VERY!
105A
11:23PM
12:30AM
WELL... ER... I... I'M CALLING IT A NIGHT!...
ALREADY?... BUT THE MOVIE'S BARELY STARTED!...
GREAT IDEA OF BILLY'S!... I HAD TO TAKE THE TV APART, BUT IT WAS WORTH IT, WASN'T IT?...
THE NEXT DAY...
WHAT IN THE...?!?... WHAT... YOU'RE ALL BROKEN OUT, OFFICER 22!!... MEASLES?... RUBELLA?...
HIVES, CHIEF!... I'M ALLERGIC TO FISH, CHIEF!!
105B

Swimming Out of Bounds

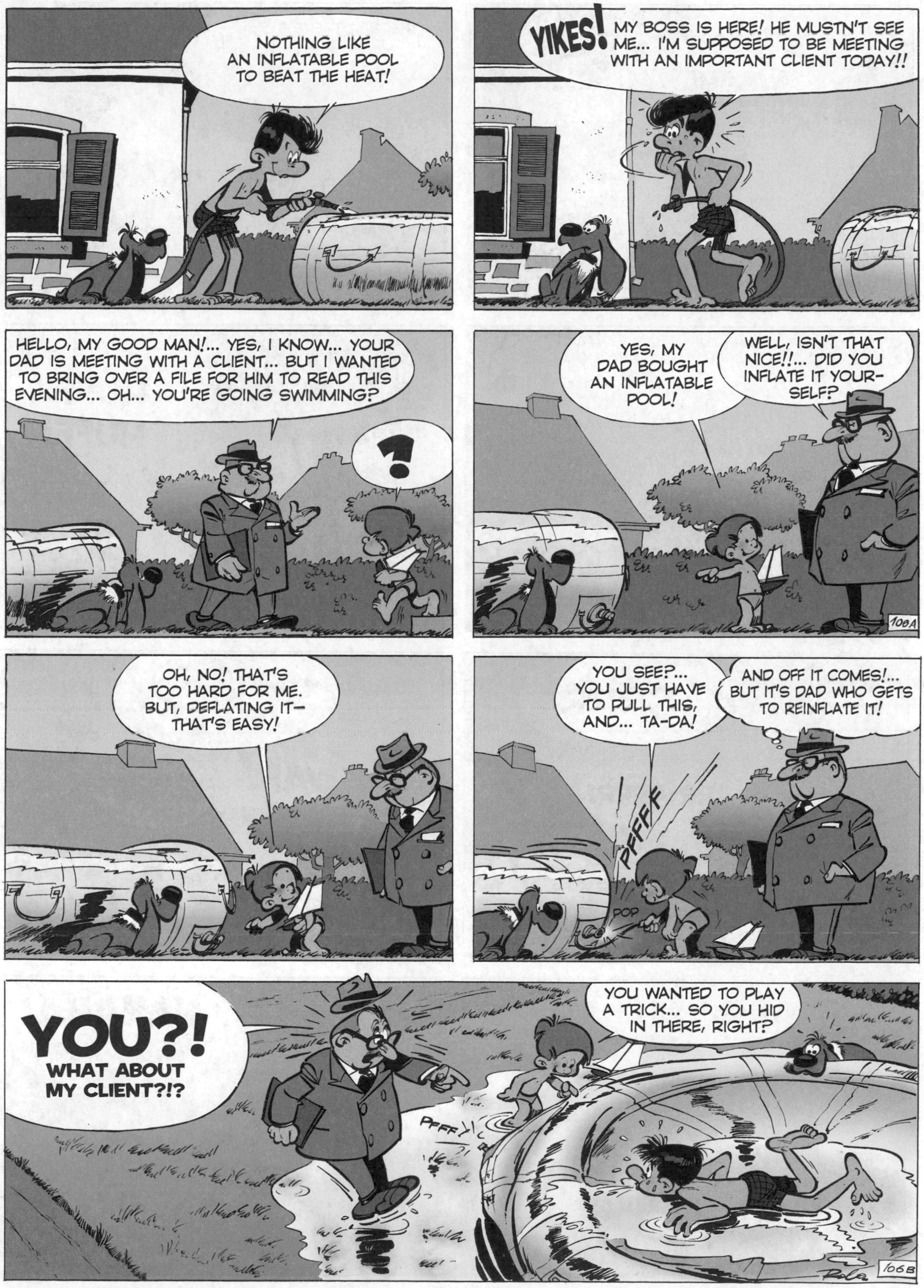
NOTHING LIKE AN INFLATABLE POOL TO BEAT THE HEAT!
YIKES!
MY BOSS IS HERE! HE MUSTN'T SEE ME... I'M SUPPOSED TO BE MEETING WITH AN IMPORTANT CLIENT TODAY!!
HELLO, MY GOOD MAN!... YES, I KNOW... YOUR DAD IS MEETING WITH A CLIENT... BUT I WANTED TO BRING OVER A FILE FOR HIM TO READ THIS EVENING... OH... YOU'RE GOING SWIMMING?
?
YES, MY DAD BOUGHT AN INFLATABLE POOL!
WELL, ISN'T THAT NICE!!... DID YOU INFLATE IT YOURSELF?
108A
OH, NO! THAT'S TOO HARD FOR ME. BUT, DEFLATING IT— THAT'S EASY!
YOU SEE?... YOU JUST HAVE TO PULL THIS, AND... TA-DA!
AND OFF IT COMES!... BUT IT'S DAD WHO GETS TO REINFLATE IT!
PFFFF
POP
YOU?! WHAT ABOUT MY CLIENT?!?
YOU WANTED TO PLAY A TRICK... SO YOU HID IN THERE, RIGHT?
PFFF
106B

My Hero

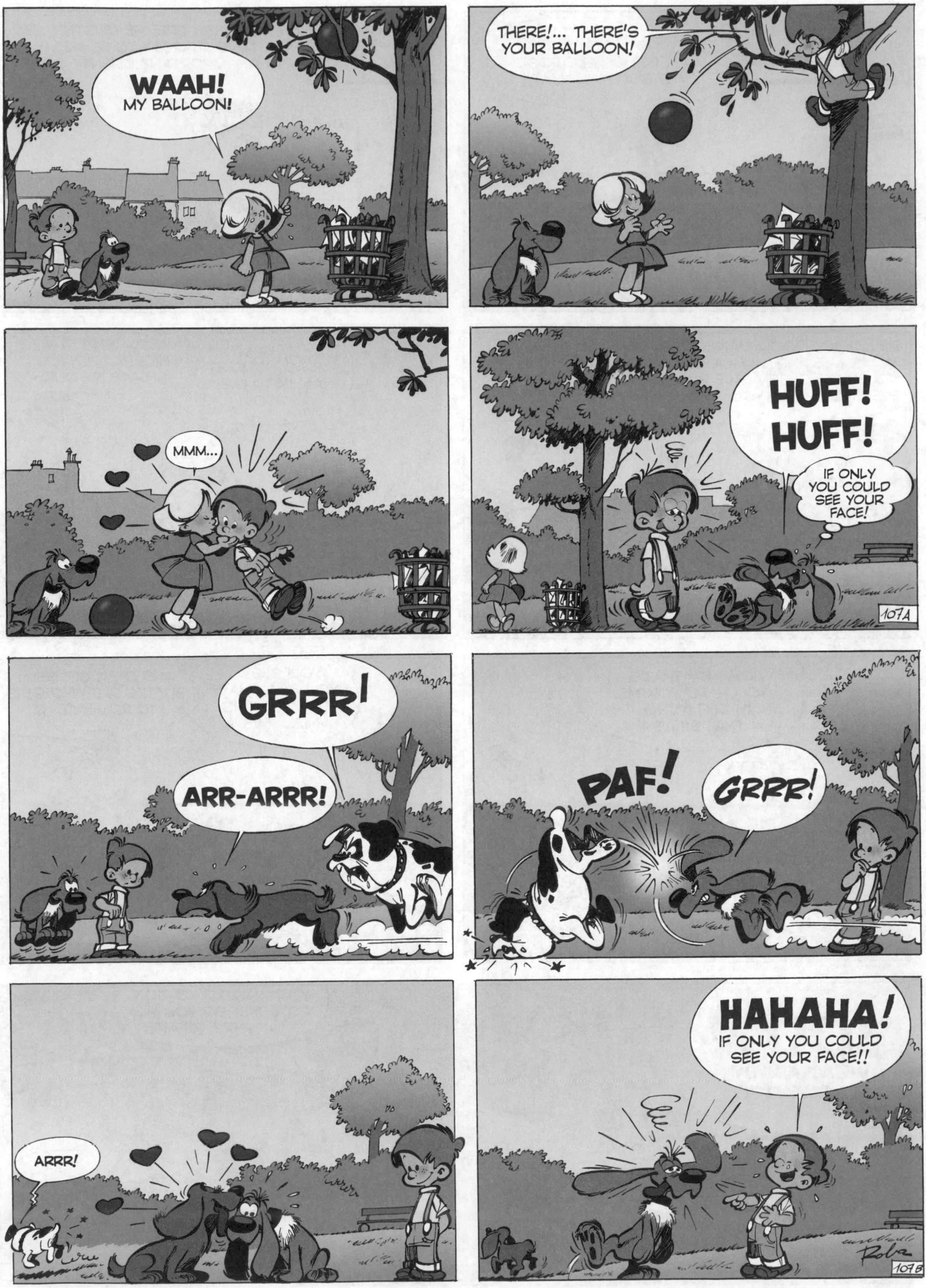

WAAH!
MY BALLOON!
THERE!... THERE'S YOUR BALLOON!
MMM...
HUFF! HUFF!
IF ONLY YOU COULD SEE YOUR FACE!
107A
GRRR!
ARR-ARRR!
PAF!
GRRR!
ARRR!
HAHAHA!
IF ONLY YOU COULD SEE YOUR FACE!!
Roba
107B

The Sounding of the Horn

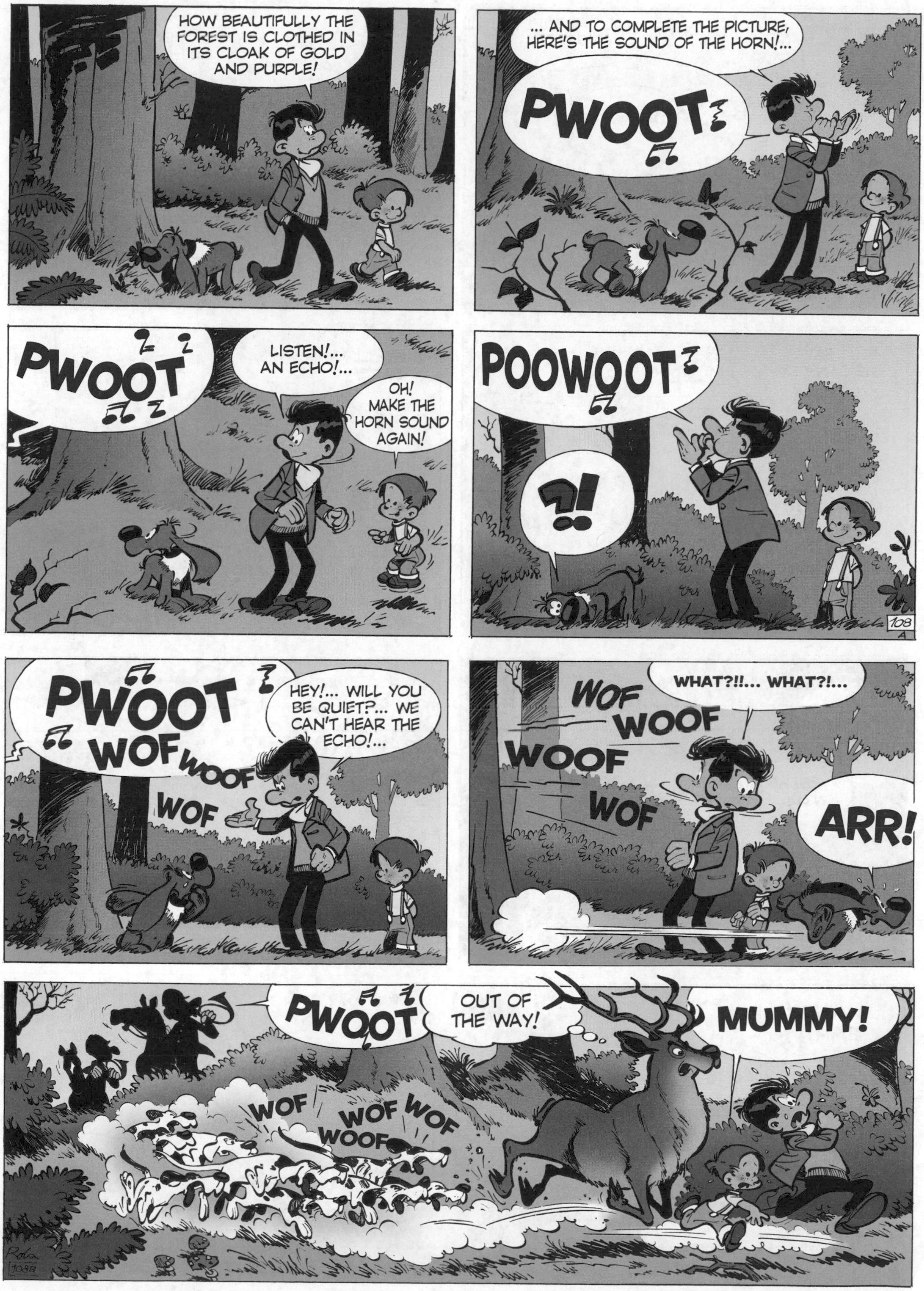

HOW BEAUTIFULLY THE FOREST IS CLOTHED IN ITS CLOAK OF GOLD AND PURPLE!
... AND TO COMPLETE THE PICTURE, HERE'S THE SOUND OF THE HORN!...
PWOOT
PWOOT
LISTEN!... AN ECHO!...
OH! MAKE THE HORN SOUND AGAIN!
POOWOOT
?!
108 A
PWOOT
WOF WOOF WOF
HEY!... WILL YOU BE QUIET?... WE CAN'T HEAR THE ECHO!...
WOF WOOF WOOF WOF
WHAT?!!... WHAT?!...
ARR!
PWOOT
OUT OF THE WAY!
MUMMY!
WOF WOF WOF WOOF

Double Agent

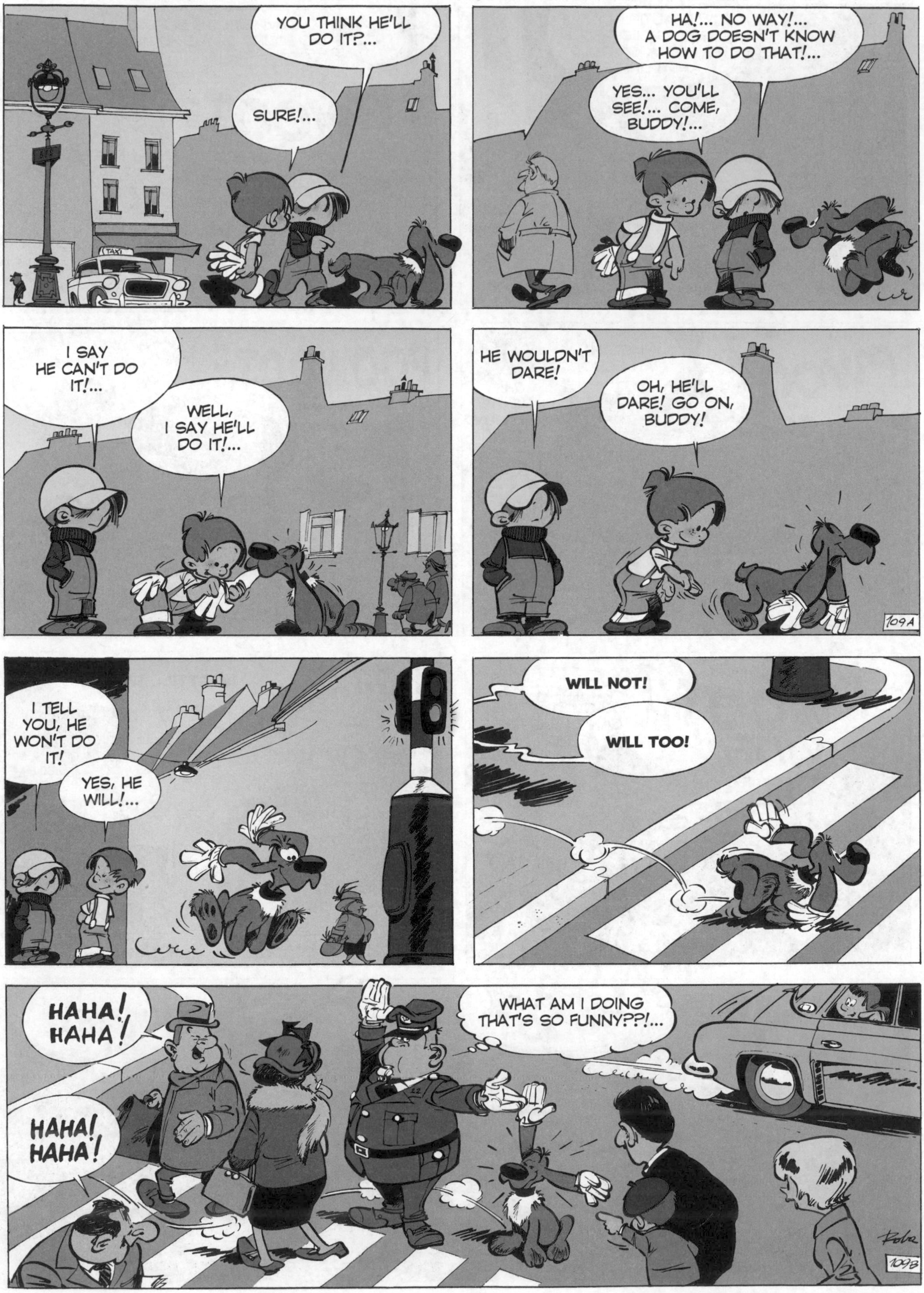
YOU THINK HE'LL DO IT?...
SURE!...
HA!... NO WAY!... A DOG DOESN'T KNOW HOW TO DO THAT!...
YES... YOU'LL SEE!... COME, BUDDY!...
I SAY HE CAN'T DO IT!...
WELL, I SAY HE'LL DO IT!...
HE WOULDN'T DARE!
OH, HE'LL DARE! GO ON, BUDDY!
109A
I TELL YOU, HE WON'T DO IT!
YES, HE WILL!...
WILL NOT!
WILL TOO!
HAHA! HAHA!
HAHA! HAHA!
WHAT AM I DOING THAT'S SO FUNNY??!...
109B

Follow the Bouncing Ball

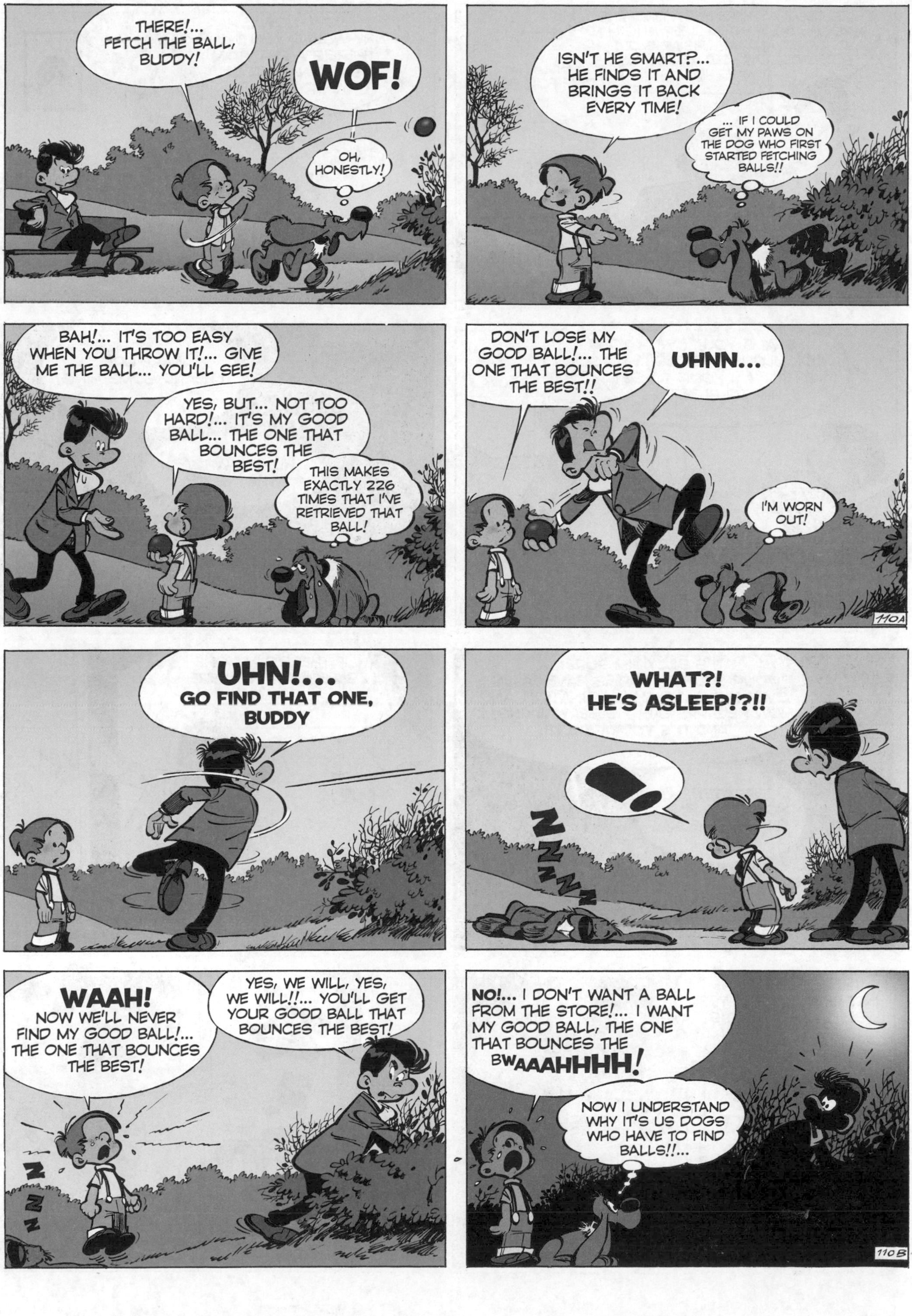
THERE!... FETCH THE BALL, BUDDY!
WOF!
OH, HONESTLY!
ISN'T HE SMART?... HE FINDS IT AND BRINGS IT BACK EVERY TIME!
... IF I COULD GET MY PAWS ON THE DOG WHO FIRST STARTED FETCHING BALLS!!
BAH!... IT'S TOO EASY WHEN YOU THROW IT!... GIVE ME THE BALL... YOU'LL SEE!
YES, BUT... NOT TOO HARD!... IT'S MY GOOD BALL... THE ONE THAT BOUNCES THE BEST!
THIS MAKES EXACTLY 226 TIMES THAT I'VE RETRIEVED THAT BALL!
DON'T LOSE MY GOOD BALL!... THE ONE THAT BOUNCES THE BEST!!
UHNN...
I'M WORN OUT!
110A
UHN!... GO FIND THAT ONE, BUDDY
WHAT?! HE'S ASLEEP!?!!
WAAH! NOW WE'LL NEVER FIND MY GOOD BALL!... THE ONE THAT BOUNCES THE BEST!
YES, WE WILL, YES, WE WILL!!... YOU'LL GET YOUR GOOD BALL THAT BOUNCES THE BEST!
NO!... I DON'T WANT A BALL FROM THE STORE!... I WANT MY GOOD BALL, THE ONE THAT BOUNCES THE BWAAAHHHH!
NOW I UNDERSTAND WHY IT'S US DOGS WHO HAVE TO FIND BALLS!!...
110B

Beware the Sleepwalker!

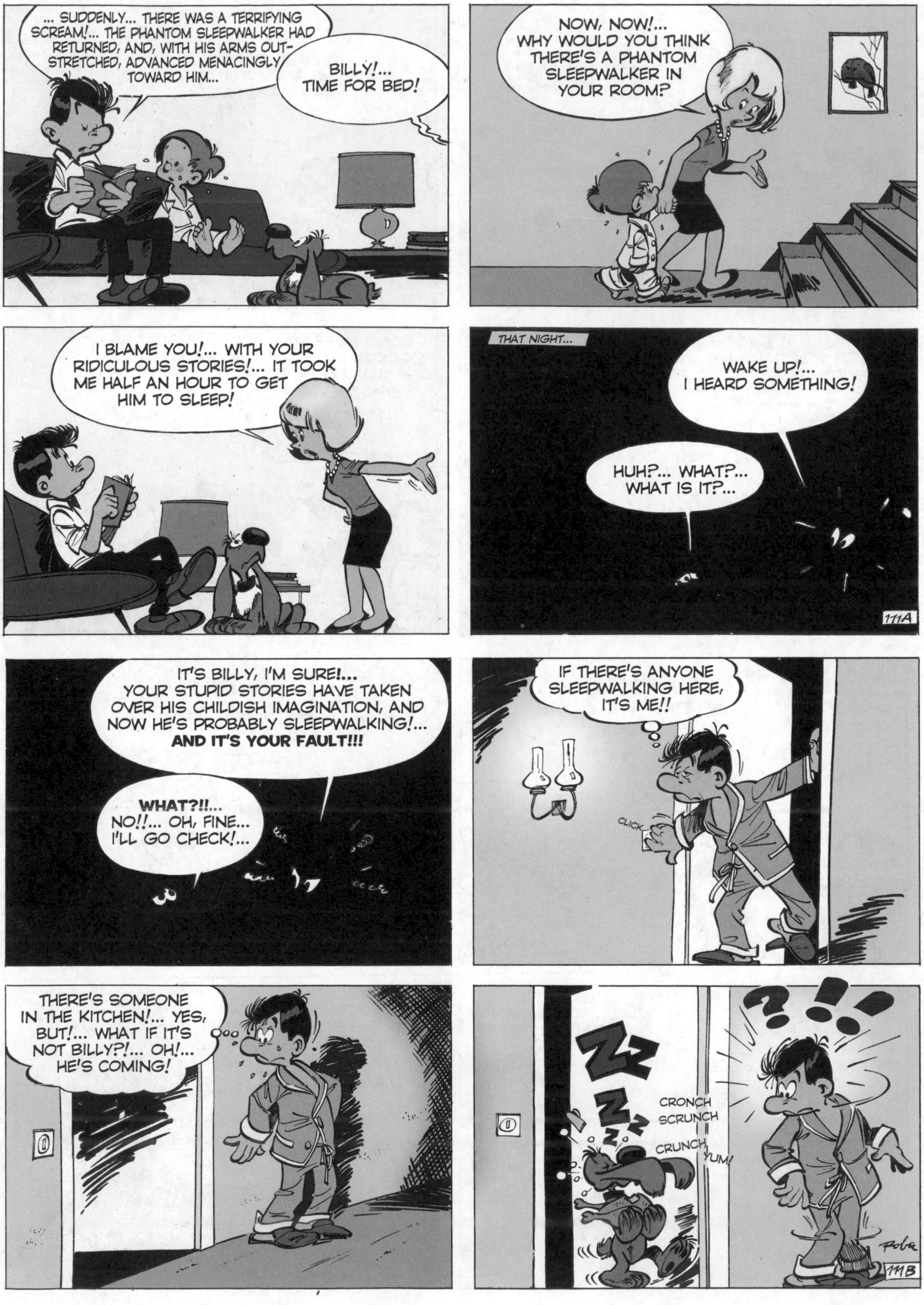
... SUDDENLY... THERE WAS A TERRIFYING SCREAM!... THE PHANTOM SLEEPWALKER HAD RETURNED, AND, WITH HIS ARMS OUT-STRETCHED, ADVANCED MENACINGLY TOWARD HIM...
BILLY!... TIME FOR BED!
NOW, NOW!... WHY WOULD YOU THINK THERE'S A PHANTOM SLEEPWALKER IN YOUR ROOM?
I BLAME YOU!... WITH YOUR RIDICULOUS STORIES!... IT TOOK ME HALF AN HOUR TO GET HIM TO SLEEP!
THAT NIGHT...
WAKE UP!... I HEARD SOMETHING!
HUH?... WHAT?... WHAT IS IT?...
111A
IT'S BILLY, I'M SURE!... YOUR STUPID STORIES HAVE TAKEN OVER HIS CHILDISH IMAGINATION, AND NOW HE'S PROBABLY SLEEPWALKING!... AND IT'S YOUR FAULT!!!
WHAT?!!... NO!!... OH, FINE... I'LL GO CHECK!...
IF THERE'S ANYONE SLEEPWALKING HERE, IT'S ME!!
CLICK
THERE'S SOMEONE IN THE KITCHEN!... YES, BUT!... WHAT IF IT'S NOT BILLY?!... OH!... HE'S COMING!
ZZZZ
CRONCH
SCRUNCH
CRUNCH
YUM!
?!!
Roba
111B